*"Cher—what's* [barcode: D0486601]
*Tai said gently.*

"No, I mean, yes, I mean, I don't know. Maybe. I miss him."

I could understand why Josh wasn't calling all that much from Paris. But why hadn't he answered my last two letters? Wasn't he missing me, too?

And then it hit me. Josh must be feeling as wretched as I do, only he can't bear to tell me and get me all upset. He doesn't want to wig me out.

Then I looked up at my friends and thought, What kind of role model am I? Brooding, mooning? This is hardly my image. I quickly recovered and, smiling brightly, said, "I'm okay. It's fine. Where should we go for dessert?"

But what about Josh?

And that's when it came to me. It's like when you pass a store window and you just know the dress in it was there because it magically knew *you* were about to walk by. It was so kismet.

My mission was clear: Josh needed me. I had to go to Paris.

# An American Betty in Paris

### A Novel by Randi Reisfeld

**AN ARCHWAY PAPERBACK**
Published by POCKET BOOKS
New York  London  Toronto  Sydney  Tokyo  Singapore

AN ARCHWAY PAPERBACK *Original*

An Archway Paperback published by
POCKET BOOKS, a division of Simon & Schuster Inc.
1230 Avenue of the Americas, New York, NY 10020

TM and copyright © 1996 by Paramount Pictures

ISBN: 0-671-56869-8

First Archway Paperback printing February 1996

10  9  8  7  6  5  4  3  2  1

AN ARCHWAY PAPERBACK and colophon are registered trademarks of Simon & Schuster Inc.

Printed in the U.S.A.

IL 7+

Okay, so like, the author is totally into thanking . . .

Fran Lebowitz of Writer's House for thinking of me, Anne Greenberg of Pocket Books, for like the same thing.

And then there are all those random generics—and you know who you are!—who like said, "You can do it!" and "I'll give you my apartment in Florida to write it!" and "No, Cher would never do that, change it!" and "This makes no sense . . ." and all that other encouraging and supportive stuff.

But duh, the most profuse and rampant *mercis beaucoup* go to my t.b.'s Marvin, Scott, Stefanie, and Peabo. Like always. With love. Totally.

# An American Betty in Paris

# Chapter 1

Chère Cher,
  Did you know your name means "dear" in French? It also means "expensive"! I'm learning so much over here. Our research project is going really well, and Paris is *très belle* (that means "very beautiful")— almost as beautiful as you are . . .

*I*t was about the bazillionth time I'd read that letter from Josh, the first he'd e-mailed since he left two months ago for a major intense work-study program at some college in Paris. I'd printed it out, along with all the others he'd sent, so I could keep them close at all times.

Josh used to be this geeky, grungy stepbrother type whose mom was married to my dad for about a nanosecond. We were like from different planets, alien beings. My friends thought he was a Baldwin, but to me . . . not even! When I used to think of him—which wasn't very often—he was more a type than a person. He was all PC and earnest and like this do-gooder for humanity. Very '60s. He used to think of me as a type, too—an empty-headed, selfish, spoiled, superficial space cadet. As if! I am a totally normal '90s teenager.

Josh had been living in Seattle but was going to college at UCLA. Which is when he started hanging around our house, Kato-like, playing couch commando with the remote, raiding the fridge, and mainly being a smart-talking pain in the butt.

But a bizarre thing happened. I was going through some weird stuff, buggin' out about the boyfriend thing. I was so capable when it came to fixing up other people but totally clueless about myself. I found myself totally obsessing about Josh. When he put me down, he actually hurt me! I even started to take what he said seriously! And then I had this like epiphany. Josh was getting to me because I was out-of-bounds crazy for him. At that same moment, he realized he loved me, too. And then it was like we were the only two people in Beverly Hills. It was way Tony and Maria in *West Side Story*.

"Paging Cher Horowitz! Will you kindly reenter earth's atmosphere? Perhaps you'd like to share what you're reading with the rest of the class?"

Mr. Hall-Geist, my debate teacher, totally horned in on my MCI moment. You'd think, after all I did for him, he could leave me alone to my excellent reverie. If it weren't for me, he'd still be the pudgy, balding, boring, miserable singleton he used to be. Okay, like he's still pudgy, balding, and boring. But at least he's not alone anymore. Thanks to my matchmaking—no brags, but that *is* one of the things I am usefully superior at—he's now actually married, to Ms. Geist-Hall, our history teacher.

"Uh, no, Mr. Hall-Geist, thanks for the opportunity, but that won't be necessary." *As if* I'd ever read Josh's letter aloud to this class of high school morons, all of whom had now been brutally awakened from their own stupors to stare at me. Good that I'd picked the checked Chanel suit with the lace camisole and platform Mary Janes.

Hall-Geist droned on. "Well, in that case, perhaps you'd like to join our discussion: Cameras in the Courtroom— Do They Help or Hamper Justice?"

I actually had a position on that issue. Like until some of those Marcia Clark–type defense attorneys learned how to dress, television audiences around the world should be spared. Therefore, cameras totally hamper justice and should be banned. I didn't get to say all that, though, because just then the bell rang.

"Sorry, Mr. Hall-Geist—I'll tell you tomorrow." I tossed my buttery leather Bolsa Chica mini backpack over my shoulder, dashed out the door, whipped out my cellular, and punched the memory button to De's number.

De—given name Dionne—is my best friend. At first we connected because we were the only two people at school who knew what it was like to have everybody want to be us. We're both full-on Bettys. I'm azure-eyed and blond; she's CCAA—Culturally Correct African-American—down to her pure silk hair extensions, golden nose ring, and slashingly bold ensembles. We are the crème de la crème of America's young, acquisitive, and hyperstylized. Through the years we have totally been there for each other through bad hair days, postal parents, and excess (though temporary) poundage pork-fests.

3

De picked up her cel on the first ring. "Zup, Cher?" It's like she can tell my ring from anyone else's, that's how close we are.

"I'm Audi to Melrose to pick up a box of those homemade granola chocolate chip cookies to FedEx to Josh. Want to come?"

"I can't." De sounded faithfully disappointed. "I'm late for my last practice lesson before I take my driver's test tomorrow. How about we go after the test? Then we can shop, and we'll have something to celebrate, too."

Driver's test. That was something I'd put out of my mind. I don't normally dwell on negativity, and that's been the one thorn in my otherwise pretty golden sixteenth year. And it's not like I shouldn't have passed. Hello? I'm a totally capable driver. But you know those days when, no matter what you do, everything's against you? Well, that was me on the day of my own test. Just because I was a little distracted—hello? I only *grazed* the side of one small pickup truck—I failed. It was the first time I'd failed at something that I couldn't talk my way out of.

Anyway, I put my whole driving thing on hold. I *so* wanted De to pass. She had a classic BMW convertible that matched our entire aura. I agreed to put off the Josh cookie thing until tomorrow and went home.

"Cher, you home?" That was Daddy, calling from downstairs. As if I hadn't said, "Hi, Daddy, I'm home," a half hour ago. But when he's holed up in his office, Daddy doesn't hear me. His powers of concentration are deeply amazing.

"Upstairs, Daddy. Be down in a sec."

"No, it's okay, I'll come up."

I live in the hills part of Beverly Hills with Daddy. He's a hugely successful litigator. He makes mountains of money by arguing other people out of theirs. He has a deeply creased forehead and thick eyebrows that kind of knit together when he's concerned. Which he was. "I just got a bill from the pool cleaners, and it looks like they're overcharging. I don't remember seeing an original estimate. I want to make sure they aren't ripping us off. Could you look for it? I think what's-her-name might've stuffed it somewhere."

Daddy was referring to Lucy, our housekeeper and my special friend. She cooks and cleans, but she's calorically challenged. So I help her in the battle of the butt-bulge. Daddy can't remember Lucy's name, but that's because he hardly sees her. She's too afraid to talk to him and runs the other way when she sees him coming.

"I'll get right on it, Daddy."

But first I had to check the computer for a letter from Josh. I'd sent him two in the past week. My screen saver was on with the Gucci bag parade scuttling across the monitor. I clicked onto the e-mail feature. But "You have no unread mail" was the only message on the screen.

Josh's environmental studies professor had hooked up with a way important researcher at a college called the Sorbonne in Paris. Together, they were doing some waterworld project, comparing and contrasting conservation methods between L.A. and Paris. Josh and three other students were the only ones in the whole class chosen to go along. It was a way prestigious opportunity. Josh couldn't possibly turn it down.

Truth is, he didn't want to. "Of course I'll miss you, Cher, but this is important. We could really do some good here." On the day Josh told me, he looked deeply into my eyes so I'd realize how much this meant to him. Josh thinks he's going to practice environmental law one day. He saw this as a chance to make a contribution to the world.

Some other girl, a clingy, whiny, insecure type, would've given Josh a hard time with it, but not me. I knew I'd miss him, but that was okay. Sometimes you have to make sacrifices for the good of the world and all that. So I was actually in favor of him going. Considering we'd been together less than a year, our relationship was so evolved already.

Our last night together was a total bliss-blitz, way romantic and bittersweet. Josh and I took my loqued-out Jeep—which I will be able to drive legally one day—and went up to Mulholland Drive, one of L.A.'s highest points. Okay, so it was all smoggy and we couldn't see the lights of the city below us, but it didn't matter. We only had eyes for each other anyway. "I'll miss you, Cher, you know that?" he'd said tenderly, his strong arms holding me close.

I buried my head in his chest, inhaled his Polo cologne, and whispered, "I'll miss you, too, Josh, but parting is such sweet sorrow." He grasped my shoulders and gently pulled me away, giving me a quizzical look. I continued, "And absence makes the heart grow fonder . . . and—"

"Where'd you hear all that?" he asked.

"It's way famous," I answered brightly, surprised to know something literary Josh didn't. And then he laughed, cupped my chin in his hand, and lifted my lips to his. *"Je t'aime,"* he said, just before he kissed me meaningfully. I didn't know what he meant, so I just murmured, "Me, too." The next morning he left.

Since Josh had been away, we'd talked—by phone, fax,

or e-mail—religiously. I told him what was going on in my life; he told me about water samples and sent books to improve my mind. He'd gotten into some French dudes named Sartre and Camus. And this Beckett guy who wasn't French but lived there. Or something.

So even though he hadn't written today, I told myself that everything was fine between us—in fact, he'd probably call tomorrow morning—and went down into the kitchen to ask Lucy about the estimate Daddy needed. At the bottom of the stairs, I did what I always do: I paused and looked up at the portrait of my mother on the wall.

My mom died when I was a baby. Everyone says I look like her, but it's kind of hard to tell from the portrait. She was a Betty, all right, but she's all poufy hair sprayed to oblivion and dressed in these vintage disco boots. Sometimes I think of her as Disco Mom. She died during a routine liposuction, is what I always tell everyone, but every once in a while I wonder if there's more no one's telling me.

I keep myself from missing her by pretending she's still here. I talk to her, keep her up to speed on my life. I've been doing it so long it's like I can sense when she approves and when she doesn't. Like I can tell she thumbs-up my relationship with Josh. It's just like Daddy and her. They were so made for each other. Not that Daddy hasn't had a parade of Bettys in his life, including Josh's mom, Gail. But no one could ever take the place of my mom. She and Daddy were each other's One True Love.

"Hey, Luce," I greeted her in the kitchen. She had her nose in the cookbook I'd given her—*The Butter-Buster's*

*Companion Cookbook*—while speed-shoving spoonfuls of Ben & Jerry's double chocolate fudge brownie into her heavily lipsticked mouth. "Lucy, I thought we were past all that," I admonished. I loved Lucy, I really did, but I was starting to think that as a project, she might just be my one big failure.

"I was just throwing it out, but there was a little left on the bottom which melt and make the garbage all wet and tear the bag. So I help by finishing it." Lucy has a rationale for everything, especially when it comes to food.

"Whatever." I sighed, deciding not to argue with her. "Daddy can't find the original estimate for the pool cleaners—you know that new company we switched to last summer? Do you remember seeing it?"

"No, I no see." Lucy scraped the last drop of ice cream from the bottom of the carton and dropped it into the garbage.

"Not there, Lucy—put it in the cardboard recycling bin, remember?" These days, our kitchen had its own recycling department: There were bins for newspapers, glass, cans, and cardboard. Josh's influence was everywhere!

If Lucy hadn't seen the bill, that meant I could eliminate the kitchen. I relocated into Daddy's office, a hugely somber wing of our house, paneled in real mahogany and lined with law books. Since Daddy had stayed upstairs, I had free rein and started with the top drawer of his desk.

It was stuffed with papers—bills, flyers, my old report cards! I never knew Daddy kept them. I kept rifling through, but no luck. I tried another drawer.

Daddy's appointment calendar from last year was on top. I couldn't imagine the estimate would be in there, but I would leave no page unturned. I pulled the calendar out of the drawer. Just as I did, something came flying out and drifted onto the floor. I picked it up. It was one of those Jurassic-era black-and-white photos with the serrated edges. It was of me as a baby.

I was about to stuff it back in, when I noticed another photo stuck to the back of it. Carefully, I separated the two. This one showed a couple. Her arms were around his neck; his were around her waist. They were looking dreamily into each other's eyes. It was . . . yes, it was my mom, only different from the portrait in the living room. I mean, younger.

I was so busy staring at my mom, I barely noticed the guy she was with. I assumed it was Daddy. But when I looked closely, something was out of whack. It wasn't Daddy. This guy had blond hair.

# Chapter 2

Melrose was jammed with traffic, but De was oblivious as she burbled on, "And parallel parking? Tscha! Smooth as my silk Vicky's Secret teddy." De was describing in ad-nauseating detail how she'd aced her driving test. "Sure, I was nervous, but I just focused. You know how Murray's always telling me to focus? Well, it all came together, and it went just like he said it would."

Murray is De's boyfriend. His look varies from year to year, as his knowledge of African culture evolves. This year, he's all dreadlocks, draggy baggies, and jive talk, the last of which drives De to distraction. (Perfect diction is a thing with her.) But when he wants to, Murray can talk to anyone about anything and make it sound convincing. He's a talk show host waiting to happen.

De and Murray have been glued at the hip since they met. They keep their relationship from getting stale by coming unglued every other minute, threatening to break up and worse. Try as I would to convince her that she could do like so much better, my arguments fell on mink-lined earmuffs.

Now De was all, "There was this one moment when I thought I'd lose it. Would you believe Murray had the nerve to beep me in the middle of my three-point turn? I was about to answer the page and tell him what a jerk he was, but it suddenly hit me that it was probably another part of the test. To see if I could concentrate. Well, my true powers of concentration won out and—"

"De, watch out!" an agitated voice from the backseat interrupted. "You just barely missed that jaywalker!" The warning had come from Tai, our new best friend—or, as we say, t.b. for true blue. Tai Frazer is classic, olive-skinned, and all Julia Ormond cascading curls from *Legends of the Fall.* Her huge doe eyes mist over every time she's happy . . . or sad . . . or confused . . . or whatever. Boys experience it as all innocence. Which is as far from reality as you can get. Tai's experienced, all right, but unfortunately, in all the wrong things. It took us several concentrated weeks to straighten her out.

See, originally, De and I had taken Tai on as a project. She'd just moved to Beverly Hills from New York, and was so completely clueless. Her idea of an outfit was whatever she'd dropped on the floor the night before, and she set her sights on all the wrong boys. Because De and I are committed to using our popularity for good causes, we just had to adopt her. Now she's just like us.

Only her ultimate choice of boyfriend wasn't our first. True, there's a serious Baldwin drought at our high school, but personally, I think she should have dipped into the population a little deeper. Right now Tai has become one with the skateboarding, Valley-speak, straight-to-video Travis Birkenstock. I tried to tell her not to get too hung on Travis, explaining, "He's okay, but he's like the frame you bowl *before* it counts," but it was hopeless. She insisted they had "lots in common." It's the last word in that sentence that bothers me.

As De had decreed, we three would spend the day on Melrose Avenue, shopping and celebrating her victory. Okay, so it was technically a school day. But in my opinion, the day you pass your driver's test? Hello? That's at least as important as Columbus Day. And they give you that one off for free. I mean, we've accepted the world is round and we're still celebrating?

In matters of shopping, it's all experience and expedience. De and I pride ourselves on both. Within ten seconds of entering any given store, we automatically know if there's anything worth committing for. If not, we're Audi before the smarmy sales help gets a chance to reek their "Can I help you, girls?" at us. But when possibilities exist, we're power shoppers. We never bother trying anything on. If we don't know what fits by now, we don't deserve our status. We simply buy the item in question in several different colors and call the store to come pick up whatever we don't want. Return policies are way liberal.

First, we went into Fred Segal's, which is a whole bunch of designer boutiques rather than one actual store. Each alcove features a different designer look. Today we were checking out the new Gaultier and Montana lines. I snagged a brutally hot reptile-patterned jumper, and De picked up a candy-colored vinyl miniskirt—something only De could or would carry off—and several dozen pairs of over-the-knee Hot Sox. Total time elapsed: six and one half minutes. Total credit card damage: in the respective four digits.

Of course my highest priority was the cookies for Josh. After picking out two pounds fresh from the Homebaked Original California Cookie Company, I gave them exact instructions on priority overseas delivery.

Our arms copiously full of shopping bags, we decided to break for the lunch thing at Johnny Rocket's. There was a wait, so Tai took the beeper they offered. Which allowed us to resume shopping until the beeper went off, alerting us that our table was ready. Such a simple, efficient concept.

Fifteen minutes later we were seated. "Passing my driver's test has put me in the mood for a calorie-fest," De declared, and went on to order her burger "broiled, medium well, no bun, no ketchup, no mayo, no onions, no relish, and could you blot the grease off before you serve it? Oh, and lettuce and tomato, no dressing, on the side." Tai's eye was on the peanut butter and jelly sandwich, but she thought better of it—she did the tuna salad, instead.

All signs pointed to a golden afternoon. I should have been in sisterly unity with De over her driving test. The outfits I'd scored were drop-dead cool, and my Josh cookie mission was complete.

But over my grilled breast of chicken hold-the-mayo salad, I realized something was bothering me. Some little voice inside my head was all, "Earth to Cher: You're not happy." But about what? I ticked off the possibilities. Was I jealous because De passed her driving test? No, De's my pal, and I certainly don't begrudge her a license—even though, since Tai had hers, too, it made my failure all the more glaring.

Was it listening to De blather on about Murray and Tai talk about Travis? Or maybe the song on the jukebox, "The Long and Winding Road"? Or maybe it was . . . ?

Wait. Go back to the song. The long and winding road . . . I didn't know who was singing, but they couldn't have said it better. Josh had been so far away for so long. Bingo! I'd hit the ickiness jackpot: I majorly, totally, furiously, brutally missed Josh. With all my heart and soul. All that stuff about parting being such sweet sorrow? Well, they got the sorrow part right.

Absence *wasn't* making my heart grow fonder—it was just making me feel all empty inside. Like when you open your closet and discover the only outfit you crave is at the cleaners. Which I totally hate.

I could understand why Josh wasn't calling all that much. There was some huge time difference that made it all but impossible. But why hadn't Josh answered my last two letters? Wasn't he missing me, too? And then it hit me. Josh must be feeling as wretched as I do, only he can't bear to tell me and get me all upset. He doesn't want to wig me out.

"Did you even hear what I said, Cher?" De's voice cut through the fog I was in. She was looking at me with a trace of annoyance. "I was totally listening," I lied. But she saw right through me and frowned. Before she got a chance to chew me out, Tai said gently, "Cher—what's up with you? Is it Josh?"

Tai was a battle-scarred veteran of heartbreak hell. It was kind of my fault. Right after her makeover, I tried to hook her up with Elton Lozoff, the lone Baldwin at the Barney convention of boys at our school. But snobby Elton decided Tai wasn't good enough for him. He wanted me instead—as if! Anyway, Tai's grieving period was profuse. But it helped her recognize my malaise for what it was.

"No, I mean, yes, I mean, I don't know. Maybe. I miss him." I started to trail off. But then I looked up at my friends and thought, What kind of role model am I? Brooding, mooning? This is hardly my image. I quickly recovered, and smiling brightly, said, "I'm okay. It's fine. Where should we go for dessert?"

But what about Josh? What could I do to show Josh I was, basically, anyway, hanging tough?

And that's when it came to me. It's like when you pass a store window and you just know the dress in it was there because it magically knew *you* were about to walk by. It was so kismet. My mission was clear: Josh needed me. I had to go to Paris.

# Chapter 3

*I* clicked into obsession mode. I'd have to work fast. Spring break, only weeks away, would be the time to go. Of course, the whole thing would be a surprise for Josh. I'd keep writing and phoning, never letting on what I was planning. And when I got there, it would be like all slow motion. Josh would turn around, and like a vision over the horizon, I'd be there in a buttery soft, flowing baby doll dress. He'd think he was dreaming—but then, arms outstretched, alarmingly slowly, I'd run toward him. It was a scene I played over and over in my head, refining it each time.

Back on planet earth, I had a lot of groundwork to cover, involving massive quantities of people. Was I up to this? Is Anna Sui Italian? Tscha! Piece of all-natural, sugarless, lo-chol, lo-cal cake. Experience had taught me to climb the highest mountain first. In this case, my personal Mt. Everest was convincing Daddy to let me go.

Okay, so De and I had taken off to New York without telling anyone. As predicted, when Daddy found out, he went postal. Good thing I was able to smooth things over by bringing back three boxes of those black-and-white cookies he's so gaga about.

But that wouldn't work twice. Skipping off to Paris without Daddy's permission was definitely not an option. What could I say that would make him allow me to go? I looked at Mom's portrait and got inspired.

On the chosen night, I left nothing to chance. I sat down to dinner in my most respectful outfit. If clothes could talk—and I actually believe they can communicate, like dolphins—this ensemble would say, "I am a level-headed, conservative young woman with direction. I do not do anything impulsively." Okay, so clothes can fudge a little. If it's for a good cause.

I'd planned the menu scrupulously. No salads, no tofu, no sprouts, nothing resembling healthy on Daddy's plate. Nothing for him to be grumpy about. I needed Daddy all mellow. So I had Lucy go whole hog on the mashed potatoes and gravy (okay, I made her use I Can't Believe It's Not Butter; just because I was buttering up Daddy was no reason to clog his arteries), meat loaf (lowest fat ground beef in the store, I'd instructed), peas and carrots overcooked to mush oblivion.

"Want to know what I did in school today, Daddy?" I began sweetly, anticipating his FAQ (most frequently asked question). Daddy's so cute. He thinks he has to grill me to show how all paternal and concerned he is. Tscha! Of course I know Daddy cares about me. I'm the most important thing in his life.

"I was just about to ask—" he began.

Perfect opening. I slid in. "Daddy," I purred, in a tone that always elicited his most parentally concerned knitted-brows look. "I've been thinking about something."

"And how much is this thought process going to cost me?" he asked in his faux-gruff, I-don't-really-mean-it-but-this-is-what-I-always-say voice.

Ignoring the question, I forged ahead. "You know how you're always saying I should get more culture? How I should get direction?" His brows went from knitted to arched.

"Well, I was thinking about where I could get some. Then in Ms. Geist-Hall's class, I learned that Paris is way cultural. All those museums and statues and old churches—and that building that leans," I threw in. Actually, I wasn't so sure about the leaning thing. My most extravagantly cultured friend, Christian, had given me a quick primer on Paris, but we'd gone off on a virtual wonders-of-the-world tangent, and now I couldn't remember what he'd said was where.

"I'd really like to broaden my horizons," I babbled on, "get away from this . . ." I searched for the right words, "provincial mentality!" I finished triumphantly, but then tacked on, "I mean, how will I ever get direction if the only place I ever go is the mall?"

Daddy looked puzzled. I could see this wasn't playing very well, so I fast-forwarded to Plan B. "Spring break is coming up, and really the only thing I'd work on would be my tan. I wouldn't learn anything, I wouldn't accomplish anything purposeful . . ." I trailed off.

Daddy, who hadn't questioned the plethora of riches on his plate but dug in gratefully, put his fork down and turned his full attention to me. "This sudden urge for culture. It wouldn't have anything to do with the fact that a certain American college student is in Paris now?"

The cholesterol and calorie fest hadn't clouded Daddy's ability to cut to the chase. But not for nothing was I his daughter. Naturally, I was prepared. "You mean . . . Josh?" I acted all surprised, as if we'd just interrupted this program for a news bulletin. "Now that you mention it, that's right, he *is* in Paris. Well, I guess if I was there, I'd have to squeeze in some time to check up on him. But I'd do that for you, Daddy—no prob."

To my surprise, Daddy got all thoughtful. "Did you know we have relatives in Paris?" he asked. "Your mother's sister, Lois, lives there with your uncle Robert and their family. Your cousins. A girl and a boy, if memory serves."

Cousins! Now, *there* was a news bulletin! Aside from scattered stepsiblings, I didn't know I had any. We weren't much into the biological relative thing, anyway. I practically had to twist Daddy's arm just to get him to talk to his own parents.

I'd never thought about my mother's family. In my mind, she existed as a star shining brightly, the center of her own universe. It was jarring to think of her with a life before us, a family besides us.

"I have cousins?"

"Let me see, what's the girl's name? I want to say Danielle. She might even be about your age."

There are times when my tough-as-nails litigator daddy lapses into Sitcom Dad, corny quips and all. But tonight was different. Tonight he was all Daddy Unplugged, no amps and no feedback, but I didn't see it getting me any closer to the airport. I needed to steer this baby back on track, when he abruptly did it for me. "Okay, Cher, I'll consider it—but only if your aunt and uncle say you can stay with them. I will not have you gallivanting around Paris the way you did in New York. I'll fax them in the morning to see if it's okay."

I jumped out of my seat and rushed over to Daddy, ready to throw my grateful arms around him, when he added, "But even if they say yes, I don't like the idea of you traveling alone."

Now, this was a path I'd already cleared—mentally at least. "Duh! Daddy, would I even *want* to go alone? I was just about to tell you, De and Tai are coming with me. Their parents have already said yes!" I *so* hated lying to Daddy, but I figured it was technically a lie only for a few days—a week at most—before I could get my t.b.'s (okay, and their parents) to turn that into truth.

Recruiting De and Tai was a job best done tête-à-tête. (I was already thinking in French, which, serendipitously, I'd just started taking.) The old, reliable cellular was not up to this.

The next day at school, during a full-period break, I searched out my quarry. I found De first. She was hanging on Murray's arm next to the stone fountain in the Quad. As I got within striking range, I could hear that my timing was off at best. De and Murray were making plans to spend spring break together. Bummer. This was going to take even more convincing than I thought. First step: separating them.

"De, I need to talk to you." I sidled up to her and whispered in a confidential tone that said, This is a no-boy-zone conversation, maybe even about topics that revolt guys most: our periods, shaving our legs, stuff that high school boys fight desperately hard to remain clueless about. On cue, Murray bolted. "I'm Audi, woman," he said, and dashed off for some male-affirmation bonding. Soon as De and I were alone, I sprung.

"What say we break away from our old boring spring-break habits and do something totally radical and trend-setting?" De looked at me skeptically. One thing about best girlfriends; They can always see right through you. But she was willing to listen. "You mean not spend the week on the beach at Baja, the way we always do?" she asked.

"You've got to think beyond Baja, best friend," I burbled. "Let's broaden our horizons this year. Let's go to . . ." And then I burst out as if I'd just thought of it. "Paris!"

"Paris!" De burst right back before I'd gotten the final *s* out. "What kind of parallel universe are you living in, Cher? We can't just up and go to France."

"Why not?" I asked, all innocence and exuberance.

"Because . . . we . . . are . . . in . . . high . . . school." She paused between each word as if I was like classified or something. "Because we are sixteen years old, and sixteen-year-old high school girls don't just jump on the Concorde because they think it might be like neat to sashay down the Champs-Elysées for a week!"

De's diatribe was having the opposite effect intended—on both of us. I had no idea what the Champs-Elysées was—maybe the French branch of the Champs store in the Beverly Center?—but it was sounding even better than I'd imagined. Not wanting to derail her train of thought, I jumped right on. "Think of it, De, all those French designers—Yves St.-Laurent, Chanel,

Lagerfeld, Cardin, they've all got boutiques there. And Paris is totally the place for Alaïa. We could snag the most clingy, fierce new wardrobes. No one would be able to compete!"

I could see I had sparked her interest. De doesn't care if she's got the most expensive ensemble, as long as it's O & O: original and outrageous. I played that card. "They've got stuff there no one's ever seen here. We'll be at least a half-season ahead of everyone." For a second, De's dancing hazel eyes lit up with possibilities. But just as suddenly, they clouded over. If the lure of couture wasn't going to do it . . .

"I don't know, Cher, I kind of promised Murray we'd spend the week together." De was doubtful, faltering, but I could tell I'd gotten one foot in the door. I pushed it in. "Oh, Murray. Of course. You guys have been together so long . . ." I started all sympathetic in the right lane but quickly swerved over three lanes, completely ambushing her from the left. "You really run the risk of his taking you for granted, you know. Think about it, you two have practically never been separated, you're always in each other's faces. One day you just start not to notice those faces."

"Cher, what are you going on about? Murray and me, we have our problems, but taking each other for granted is not one of them," De countered, sounding not the least bit convinced. I could see this was a concept new to her. I went in for the kill. "Remember when we went to New York? Remember how much he missed you, couldn't think about anything but you? Think of what a week on another continent will do! He'll be falling all over himself waiting for you to get back—especially when you return looking like a total hottie in your new clothes. Murray won't know what hit him. Better, he won't know what to do for you first. You know that crystal drop necklace you've been eyeballing? Do you think he *won't* be meeting you at the airport with it, just 'cause he missed you so much?"

That did it. De was a goner. She morphed over completely to my side. "We'll have to convince your mom, of course," I reminded her.

She looked at me as if she'd just reentered earth's atmosphere. "You're right, Cher. And she's still getting over New York."

"Don't worry, De, we'll come up with something."

At that moment, the warning bell rang. "Gotta go. I have Hall-Geist," I said.

"Cher—wait a minute." De stopped me. "You haven't said one word about Josh. He's the real reason for the Paris push, isn't he." It was a statement, not a question. If De had just realized she'd been bamboozled, she didn't make a thing out of it. Once committed, De is solid. It's what the best friendships are based on.

I caught up with Tai after school. She was out by the west portal with Travis. I was less than joyful to find them together: Travis is much harder to get rid of than Murray. The 411 on Travis: totally two-dimensional. A bona fide boardie; not much bummed him out. Nuance and innuendo were towns in the Valley to him. Travis always had a dopey smile on his face; he couldn't say why.

Best to be straightforward and purposeful. "Tai, I need you. Can I talk to you alone?"

"Sure, okay," she said, without making the slightest move away from Travis.

"Let's do a lap," I suggested. I had to take another

route with Tai. Much as she'd evolved, the lure of couture was not getting *her* to Paris. An appeal to her sense of gratitude was the better bet. Tai was still grateful that De and I had taken her on and then rescued her from New York. Not that it was something we ever reminded her of, but she knew she owed us big time. So I was straight with her.

"Tai, remember in Johnny Rocket's? How you alone read my mind? How you knew I was missing Josh? I've decided to go . . . to visit Josh, that is. Over spring break. Only Daddy won't let me go unless you and De come, too. She's already said yes. I need you, Tai, to come with us."

"Paris? You mean in France?" Tai's geographic expertise surprised me.

"I know this is above and beyond the call, Tai," I said, hoping to jolt her into the realization that like so was New York.

"Gee, I don't know Cher, that's a pretty far-out idea." Tai still used expressions that were so five minutes ago. She needed to be taken all the way there.

"Tai, we've done a lot for you," I started. Then suddenly she got it.

"What am I thinking? I'm such a tard! Of course I'll go, Cher. You and De . . . you guys! You've done so much for me. Where would I be without you?"

We hugged. "And don't worry," I told her, "I'll help you figure out how to handle your mom."

My next event in the Paris Olympics: getting excused from class assignments due. Critical because I refuse to let my grades slip. Ever. Academic excellence is something I totally pride myself on.

Hall-Geist was handing out assignments to be completed over spring break. Mine was to prepare an oral on Freedom—a Right or a Privilege? I raised my hand. "Mr. Hall-Geist?"

"Yes, Cher," he said wearily. I think he knew what was coming next.

"My topic? That's not an issue I'll be able to give the full attention it so richly deserves." In my most grave tone I added, "And it's way too important not to."

"And why not, may I ask?"

"As it turns out, I'll be out of the country during spring break." The rest of the class looked at me, hugely impressed, as I continued. "But may I suggest a substitute? Since I'll be in"—I paused for effect—"Paris" (a collective awe came over the room), "I thought I could do my oral on a vital subject."

"And what would that subject be, Cher?" Hall-Geist wasn't nearly as harsh as he used to be, but he wasn't letting me off that easily, either.

"Well, I couldn't say yet. But I'm sure I'll find it when I'm there. And when I do, I'll broaden the whole class's horizons while I'm broadening mine." I finished with an appropriately broad smile.

"The only thing you'll broaden over there is your butt, Cher." And in this corner: Amber Salk, the wanna-Betty who stubbornly refuses to admit her overwhelming envy. In her ongoing misguided attempts at copying me and De, Amber was always changing her hair. This week she'd gone for Courteney Cox in *Friends* but ended up all Courtney Love in Hole. You'd think now that she had an actual boyfriend of her own—and didn't she and spectacularly superficial Elton totally deserve each other?—she'd get a clue.

"At least there's room on mine for expansion," I shot back. "You already need a jacket in double-digit sizes to cover yours up."

Elton Lozoff's tanned, muscular arm punched its way into the atmosphere. Hall-Geist nodded in his direction, knowing—how could he not?—that the contribution Elton was about to make had nothing to do with debate or my trip.

"Can I be excused? Tickets to the Cranberries concert are going on sale in like"—Elton consulted his Tag Heuer watch—"two hours, and I have to get in touch with my father for seat preferences." Hall-Geist brutally rebuffed Elton's request.

"I, for one, would like my horizons broadened, Mr. Hall-Geist." New county heard from: Travis, who obviously had not yet been alerted that my trip included Tai. "I vote that we let Cher go."

"It isn't up for a vote, Mr. Birkenstock, but as always your input is noted," Hall-Geist said patiently.

In the end, Hall-Geist agreed, on the condition that my oral be well-researched and on an important subject.

In English class I promised Mrs. Kalfus I'd compare and contrast our required reading lists with that of a typical high school's in France. "I'll be learning a foreign language, too," I tossed in.

Amber and her jealousy knew no boundaries: "To you, Cher, *English* is a foreign language."

I shot back. "While *your* talent is making your inadequacies obvious in any language. You are so globally impaired, Ambu-lard."

It didn't shut her up. "Mrs. Kalfus," she whined, "I don't think it's fair that Cher gets out of doing her term paper. She's not going on some cultural quest. She's going because her boyfriend's there." Then Amber narrowed her overly made-up beady eyes and went for a direct hit. "Give it up, Cher. I'll bet by now he's forgotten all about you. He's in college, he's got all of Paris at his feet. Why would he sit around and pine for a little high school girl like you? Even your precious Josh isn't that pathetic. Ever heard the expression Out of sight, out of mind? You're not even a speck in his peripheral vision anymore."

Amber thought she'd gotten me. Not even! She wasn't getting the last word. I turned to the class. "Who am I to argue with an expert dumpee? Whatever, Amber . . ." I made the W sign.

Luckily, Mrs. Kalfus had looked out the window and gotten distracted by a couple making out in the Quad. She wasn't paying attention to either me or Amber. Her decision in my favor stood.

# Chapter 4

*I* got so caught up in the pure joy of negotiating, De teased that I'd almost forgotten the real reason I was going to Paris. Not even! But every once in a while, a few days might go by before I realized I hadn't checked for new mail from Josh. Since that gap of two weeks ago, he'd been pretty good about communicating. Now it wasn't how often he was writing, it was what he was saying. His letters were getting less lovey-dovey and more informational. Like one last week: "They are keeping me so busy! We've been doing fieldwork the past three days, going to small towns around Paris to test samples . . ." He fully expounded on everything. It was almost as if he was doing a term paper.

But he couldn't fool me. I knew what Josh was doing: filling his letters with details, so I wouldn't realize how heartbroken he was. I kept mine brief, so he wouldn't suspect.

Once I'd gotten De and Tai to agree, the rest went like clockwork. Daddy had heard back immediately from Aunt Lois and Uncle Robert. They were so thrilled he'd faxed them, they invited everyone over.

Because we now had a safe and solid place to stay, Tai's and De's parents put up less of a struggle. Of course, our strategies in dealing with them were worked out ahead of time.

De lived with her mom, Carolina, a way important PR executive and one of the first African-American women to climb the brutal ladder of Hollywood success in a nongratuitous, important way. Because Carolina is hugely driven, we knew her sweet spot. We promised to check out the real box office receipts for her biggest client's new movie and to suss out potential foreign talent. She beeped us with the go-ahead.

I thought Tai's mom would be the mega challenge. It wasn't only the New York sidebar so fresh in her mind, it was also something I never think about—money. Tai's family wasn't exactly rolling in it. They lived in the flats part of Beverly Hills. It was way Brenda and Brandon when they first moved to 90210. Their friends were all frothy-rich while their dad was an accountant to the rich.

But as it turned out, Tai's mom's new boyfriend—an extremely possible stepdad-to-be for Tai—was a network correspondent bucking for anchor status. He was actually in favor of the trip. He even said Tai could use his airline mileage points so she could fly free. "I've been all over the world, girls," he spoke brightly, enunciating as if reading from a TelePrompTer, "and as I keep reminding Tai, it's important to open your eyes to all the world's cultures. We live in a global village, you know."

We hugely agreed and assured him of our eagerness to become village people.

Getting ready for the trip was major. Luckily I have natural aptitude in organizational skills. I started with two major checklists labeled Home and Abroad. Under Home was all the stuff I would have done that week if I'd actually been home. Namely, taking care of Daddy. I made his dentist appointment and lined up the chauffeur to make sure Daddy didn't bail. I saw that he was due for his bimonthly chiropractor visit. Daddy's disks are chronically in need of rearranging. I set up a home visit.

One night I was up later than usual, sprawled on the king-size, organizing Daddy's vitamins by color, shape, and potency, and his breakfast menus into red zone notevers (eggs, butter, anything gooey) and green zone okays (fruit, cereal, skimmed milk). I'd just gotten up to search for the remote when the phone rang. Assuming De or Tai, I did auto-pilot. "Zup, girlfriend?"

"Cher? Is that you?"

Josh! He so rarely called anymore that for a second I thought it might be Elton, playing a joke on me. But Josh's deep, soothing voice was unmistakable. Not wanting him to detect my surprise, I said lightly, "Of course it's me, silly. Who else would be answering my phone at this hour?"

"Sorry, I know it's late, but I was hoping to catch you up. It's real early here, and I'm just leaving for another field trip. I wanted to thank you for the cookies. That was so thoughtful of you."

Thank me for the cookies—as if that was the real reason he was calling! Josh misses me so much, he got up before the crack of dawn to call. "They're really keeping us on the go," he continued. "I almost never get a chance to call anymore. We've gotten involved with Greenpeace. It's an international environmental organization. My group is away for these overnights, and by the time I get back, I'm too bushed to do anything except sleep." He sounded anything but tired—perky, in fact. Then his voice got low, and he went all conspiratorial and romantic. "So how are you, Cher . . . I mean, how are you *really?*"

I couldn't allow myself to be lured into a mushy conversation. What would that accomplish, besides making him feel even more lonely? What if I ruined his day or, worse, the project he was working so hard on?

"Up late studying?" he guessed.

"Umm, yeah, burning that midnight oil." It wasn't exactly a lie.

Suddenly we were brutally interrupted. "Josh! Are you ready?" The voice in the background was generically female—and whiny. "The group is leaving, Joshie, come on!"

Joshie?? What was *that?*

"I'm sorry, Cher, I gotta go—I thought I had a few more minutes to talk to you. I'll call as soon as I can."

"It's okay, Josh, really. I—" Love you, I was about to say, but the phone went dead before I got the rest out. No biggie, soon I'd tell him—that is, show him—in person.


De, Tai, and I worked on our Abroad checklists together, which we divided into sections covering our three most important areas: body, mind, and soul.

To prepare our bodies, we shopped.

To prepare our minds, we zoned in on literature. We had the bookstore deliver the basics: the Michelin guide and books by famous French authors like Danielle Steel and Jacqueline Susann. Rampantly practical De was deep into *The Chic Shopper's Guide to Paris,* topped off with a stack of *Elle* and *Marie Claire* magazines.

"Okay, soon as we get there," she said, "we find some street called Rue du Faubourg St.-Honoré. That's where Versace is."

"Are you sure? That sounds like a weird place for Versace," Tai opined.

*"Rue* means 'street,' Tai, and *du* means 'of the.' So Rue du Faubourg St.-Honoré would mean something like 'honorable street where the Faubourgs live.'" The con- nection to Versace was just beyond my grasp, but since De was already in French 2, we bowed gratefully to her expertise.

For our souls, we scheduled bikini waxes and aromatherapy sessions, and made appointments with our personal trainers and masseuses. A supple and relaxed body makes for a calm and collected soul. It's way Zen.

Each day at school, we beeped each other with pop quizzes: "Okay, how do you say, 'Do you have that in mauve?'" De asked.

"Oy-vey voos cela in . . . mauve?" I tried my best to mimic De's accent.

She was jubilant. "You go, girl!"


Our friends graciously involved themselves in our preparations. It was way vicarious. Christian came to imbue us with culture. Christian Stovitz is one of my closest confidants. Eons ago I thought we might make the perfect couple. We seemed to be on the same page in *Vogue* and *W.* But it was all wrong. When I figured out why, it led me to Josh. Now Christian's one of my most capable friends and fiercest shopping partners. Christian is not only the most magnificently attired creature in the Quad, his knowledge of all things art is mammoth.

Of course Christian knew the real reason for the Paris fling—he's as much the romantic as any of us—but he insisted we fulfill a culture quotient, too. He brought over a stack of guidebooks, a CD-ROM Virtual Paris tour and appointed himself Culture God. Opening to a page in a book called *The Best of Paris's Artistic Attractions,* he began to read. " 'There are four museums you absolutely cannot miss. First, the Louvre.' " When Christian got onto something, he could not be distracted.

". . . and the nineteenth century Impressionists are in the Musée d'Orsay—you can see some real Monets there . . . Dionne! You're not paying attention."

"I *so* appreciate this art history lesson, Mr. Christian." De enunciated clearly so there'd be no mistaking her meaning. "But with all due respect, unless these museums have runways, models, and price tags, I'm Audi before I get in."

Christian would not be quelled. "Don't be so single-minded, De. You can't go to Paris and not take in the great works of art. Global impairment is *not* what becomes a Betty most."

Murray, who sporadically sat in on these sessions, chimed in menacingly, "You sayin' there's something impaired about my woman?"

De shot him an I-don't-need-your-help-to-defend-me look and clarified, "The only guidebooks I need are those that guide me straight to designer showcases. When I return from Paris, it's my wardrobe that's going to be improved. My mind is just fine as it is."

I'm not sure why Murray insisted on being there,

anyway. He acted like a grouch potato, brooding and offering up stinging commentaries. Like when I mentioned needing an extra suitcase for my Evian bottles—I mean, Josh was there inspecting *bad* water samples. How could I afford to take a chance? Murray was all, "You don't take Evian to Paris, Cher. Where do you think it comes from?"

Travis also inflicted himself upon us with increasing frequency these days. He'd taken the news of Tai's departure hard—or as hard as this straggly-haired visitor from another planet could. The memory of Tai's sudden departure to New York was still fresh in his mind. He didn't want to lose her again.

It was actually Travis who reminded us—in a roundabout way of course—of something we'd almost forgotten. "My guidance counselor said skateboarding might be my passport to a new world of exciting opportunities."

"Passports! Oh my god! You guys! We forgot to get passports!" When Tai suddenly realizes something, her eyes open wider than a Sub-zero fridge. I noticed that she'd finally learned to put on eyeliner correctly.

But she was right about the passports. We'd never needed them before. I mean, New York was totally a foreign country, but they didn't make you show proof of citizenship to get in.

"If we hurry, we can make Moto Photo before it closes," Tai rushed on, grabbing her bag and heading for the door.

As if! Moto Photo! De and I exchanged will-our-work-on-her-*ever*-be-done? looks. And then, as only t.b.'s can, we had the exact same thought at the exact same moment.

*  *  *

A funny thing happened when we went for our passport photos. Naturally, we'd booked Herb Ritts. L.A.'s foremost fashion photographer—and a client of De's mom—is the only one who could possibly do us justice. But when Herb, sounding suspiciously like a high school yearbook photographer said, "Smile and think of your boyfriend," I didn't think of Josh. The picture that came into my mind instead was the one of my mom and that guy.

Which totally trashed the look I was going for, which was worldly-wise and jaunty. Instead, in my passport photo, I just look clueless.

# Chapter 5

*I*'d programmed my computer to help decide which outfits to take and the right pieces of luggage for them. I finally narrowed it down to twenty-five or so ensembles, each with its own set of matching accessories, including jewelry, vests, thigh-highs, berets, belts, and scarves. There were two suitcases for shoes, sandals, and boots.

As I was furiously packing, Daddy came into my room. He surveyed the mile-high piles of clothes and accessories on the floor. "Do you really think that's enough, Cher?"

"Duh, Daddy, of course not. I still have my makeup bags to drag out."

Daddy sighed loudly, shook his head, and relocated on my king-size. Red alert: He never does that unless he has something of national security importance to impart.

"Before you go, I want you to know something about your aunt and uncle."

"I'm all ears, Daddy." I sat down on the bed next to him. I thought he might break into some highly confidential files—that would be unusual in itself, since Daddy and I stay away from topics of a personal nature that might raise his blood sugar level. That's why I couldn't ask him about the photo of mom I'd found.

Daddy didn't break with tradition. He did a brief 411. Lois was my mother's older sister. Robert, her husband, a French citizen doing business in the U.S., was in international banking and way important. A few years after my cousin Danielle was born, Uncle Robert got transferred back to Paris, where they'd lived ever since. David was born there a few years later. Uncle Robert was like in charge of a bazillion employees and responsible for the banking business in all of France. Or some of it. Whatever.

I took that to mean he was massively financial, like my dad.

"Do you know them really well?" I asked with genuine curiosity.

"I used to, but you know how it goes, with the years and the distance, we've drifted apart." His eyes started to get that unplugged faraway look, but he snapped back into reality before I could press further. "They're really excited that you're coming," he added, and got up to leave. "I've got work to do. And, Cher?"

"Yes, Daddy?"

"Don't overdo it with the packing, okay?"

I wondered if there was more he wasn't saying. Like what does distance have to do with anything? Daddy has business associates he speaks to daily in China. Even I know that's farther than Paris.

The night before we left I dreamt about my mother. I used to do that a lot, but it hadn't happened much lately. So I was kind of surprised. In my dream, I was telling her all about my trip. I expected she'd be all happy, but instead, she put her arm around me protectively and said, "Be careful what you ask for, Cher. You just might get it." Huh? I had no idea what she meant, so I looked up at her quizzically. She was about to explain when I woke up. Or that is, I brutally crashed into the consciousness zone due to a clashing cacophony of sound. It seemed to be coming from the nightstand next to my bed: the phone.

"Cher Horowitz! This is your wake-up call!" It was De, buzzing me at some prehistoric hour. Then I looked at the clock. Whoops, my bad. I had totally overslept.

"You've got two hours. We're picking you up at seven." De was in her take-charge mode and sounded significantly organized. "Be ready, Cher. You cannot be fashionably late for a plane. It's going to take off with or without you."

"I was just closing my last suitcase," I mumbled unconvincingly.

"Whatever, Cher—just be ready."

At seven precisely, the bell rang. Lucy let De and her chauffeur in. Carolina was lending us her personal limo to get to LAX. Tai was already safely tucked inside.

While the chauffeur was loading my luggage into the limo, I started to give Lucy last-minute reminders about Daddy's vitamins and how to hollow out his bagels. But she bolted as soon as Daddy came down. He was way underemotional about my leaving but did hand me a new credit card, accepted at ATMs worldwide. In his faux-gruff voice he said, "You're going to a foreign country. The three of you stay together at all times. And give my regards to your aunt and uncle."

I'm not exactly sure why, but the last thing I did before I left was run upstairs and stash the ancient snapshot of my mom and that guy into my leather Tignanello backpack.

I sank into the plush vinyl Air France first-class lounge chair, checking my momentary guilt about Tai being back in coach, which was as far as the frequent flyer mileage took her. "We'll do a sporadic lap back there, so she won't feel left out," I decided, and started flipping through a copy of *Allure*.

But De wasn't thinking about Tai or even the fabulous French fashions that awaited. Now that we'd settled onto the plane, her thoughts recklessly speed-raced back to Murray.

"Can you believe he's still going to Baja without me?" De demanded indignantly.

"What else should he do, De? It is spring break for him, too. Besides, what's your problem?"

"Murray, in Baja, without me? Hello? What if he does something hyper brain-impaired—like get a tattoo or something?"

"Don't you know anything about psychology, De? Murray will be feeling so guilty and worried about what you'll think, there's less than zero chance he'd do something radical when you're away. He'll be too obsessed with you. He'll be all, 'What would De think, what will De say when she gets back?' I'll bet he's frantically

39

trying to beep you now." Since we were wireless on the plane, we'd never know.

De would not be diverted from the Murray train. "Maybe I shouldn't have gone. Maybe this was a bad idea." She was venturing into dangerously regretful waters. And it was definitely too soon for that to happen.

Partly to distract her, I suggested dipping into the population to see how Tai was faring back in coach.

Depending on how you looked at it, Tai either wasn't doing badly at all, or, slash, it had the makings of a complete disaster. Too-friendly Tai was already mixing it up with the easily-pandered-to crowd.

"You guys!" Tai greeted us. "These guys are going to Paris, too!" She actually said that as if it were a revelation (hello? the plane is going to Paris, where else would they be going?), insisting we meet Jeremy, Damon, Bailey, Charisma, and Kate—all of whom wore their "rich children of hippies" aura like a badge of honor. "They're on a European teen tour, and they brought some panoramic music."

So it seemed. We'd reached our cruising altitude of thirty-five thousand miles, and Tai's new friends had reached theirs, too. They were singing and dancing in the aisles, oblivious to the daggers being thrown at them from the other passengers.

"Stay and party with us?" Tai asked.

As if! Thanking her for the offer, De and I darted gratefully back to the serenity of first class, where De mellowed, put her headphones on, and was soon lost in the world of Coolio and TLC.

I pulled out a sheaf of Josh's letters from my backpack. Okay, so I'd already memorized all of them, but I pored over them again. Lately they had more to do with reading lists than *l'amour,* but improving me was always Josh's way of showing how much he loved me. He'd recommended some Beckett dude, saying he was almost as existential as *Ren & Stimpy.* And it wasn't as if I was ignoring Josh's recommendations. I'd devoted an entire Saturday night to *Waiting for Godot.* But after fifty pages, even I realized this Godot dude wasn't going to show. I stuck with it, though. If Josh was going all global, I didn't want to be left behind.

I wonder what Josh is doing at this exact moment? Probably taking test tubes and filling them with water samples, looking for microscopic bugs. Or maybe he's in his dorm room, writing to me. But no letter or phone call could take the place of his slightly crooked smile, the way he can look into my soul with his deeply sincere eyes, his strong, muscular arms encircling me and holding me close. And then there's his kiss. Josh had given me some of the best in all teendom. More of which awaits me, just on the other side of this ocean we're winging over.

De and I fell asleep, heads on each other's shoulders.

# Chapter 6

*T*hat's her! Maman, that's her—"

The last words I heard before everything went black seemed to be coming from a little boy on a sugar high. They were punctuated by the high-pitched yapping of a very small dog. Suddenly, I was totally surrounded and utterly vanquished by flinging arms, heaving bosoms, wet lips, and what might have been a wet canine nose. Help! I'm being squashed into oblivion. My last thought was that my cocoa silk blazer was totally wrinkling.

"Let her go! She's suffocating!" A deep, booming male voice. The army of body parts slowly disentangled and loosened their grip on me. I came to and tried to assess. My entire French family had come to the airport. And they'd brought the dog.

It's not like I had actual expectations of what they'd look like. But if I did? It wouldn't have been this.

"Cher? I am your aunt Lois." She was smiling and

crying at the same time. Aunt Lois, who didn't carry a bag, accessorized with a tiny Chihuahua named Gigi in the crook of her arm. "You are so beautiful! I'd know you anywhere!" she gushed in perfect English. Duh, she was American, what did I expect?

"And I am your uncle Robert." The voice that had saved me from an untimely death by suffocation broke in. He pronounced it "Ro-bear," and I could see why. He was massively tall and massively grizzly—but not like the bear that wounded Brad Pitt in *Legends of the Fall.* More like the one in July on my teddy bear calendar—furry, round, friendly.

Uncle Robear extended his hand. "You have no idea how thrilled we are that you are here." Just then we heard a comforting and familiar sound, the ring of a cellular. Reflexively, De and I dug into our bags. It took a minute before our jet-lagged minds realized, hello? We didn't bring them because Murray, in his exasperated, how-clueless-can-you-be tone said they wouldn't work in Paris. It was Uncle Robert's that had gone off.

Aunt Lois rushed to fill the momentary conversational void. "And this is Danielle, your cousin." She beamed at the girl on her left, who took a confident step toward us. "Everyone calls me Dani," she said, with an enough-to-be-cute trace of an accent. Everything about Dani was cute and bubbly, but on her it worked. She was petite but not without curves. Her chestnut hair was long, thick, and wavy. Even her bangs were bubbly. They didn't sit flat on her forehead but rounded as if covering a speed bump. Her eyes were cornflower blue and clear.

Dani was wearing a plaid miniskirt, over-the-knee-highs, a starchy button-down oxford shirt, and a tweed jacket. Lose the shirt, I thought, already having regained enough of my composure to start considering a makeover . . . stop. Josh is right. I have to accept people as they are, not try to make everyone better. Remind me again of why?

"*Maman,* what about me?" The little boy voice. I looked over—it came from the sweetest face I'd ever seen. Dark complexion, huge dark eyes, with the kind of long, curly, thick eyelashes that are so wasted on boys, they should be declared illegal. A Baldwin-to-be. I fell in love with cousin David on the spot.

Dani took a step forward and extended her hand. "You must be De and Tai."

As De and Tai did the charmed-to-meet-you thing, Uncle Robert, who'd wrapped his phoner, vigorously shook their hands and took charge. "*Allons-y,* let's go. The airport is no place to get acquainted."

I hadn't pictured where my French family would live, but obviously, I expected acreage. Unless you counted the leafy trees out front, there was nothing green in sight. The high-rise apartment building was similar to the ones in New York. I flashed on the possibility that Daddy had been wrong. Maybe they weren't so financial after all. Until I saw the apartment.

An oasis of vanilla, it was all white overstuffed sofas, marble-topped coffee tables, and recessed lighting. Sheer curtains framed double-height doors. A white baby grand piano was riddled with family photos. I made a mental note for closer examination later.

We were all massively relieved, but Tai was the only one who sputtered, "Wow! I didn't know apartments came in this size! It's like a whole house on one floor."

Aunt Lois put one maternal arm around Tai and the

other around De. "Come, I'll show you around. Will it be okay if you and Dionne share a room?" Once De and Tai saw the size of the room—like, you could have parked De's Beemer, my Jeep, and even Tai's '70s-mobile in it— they assured her they had no prob and followed Aunt Lois for the grand tour.

"Dani, take Cher to your room—the cousins will stay together." She beamed.

Jet-lagged though I was, I understood that the reason for bunking me with Dani wasn't because the apartment was bedroom-challenged. The idea was engineered so we could get to know each other. Normally, I'd want to handle the unpacking of my personal possessions myself, but maybe Dani could learn something by getting a close-up of my stuff.

As we were transferring shoes and boots from my suitcase to one of her closets, I asked all casually, "Do you know how far the Sorbonne is from here?"

Dani seemed surprised by my question. It probably wasn't the first thing she expected me to ask. "Are you thinking of maybe going to university here? That would be so cool!" She accented the word *cool*.

"Well, it's a long way off, but I don't want to leave any stone unturned. Educationally, that is," I answered. I wasn't sure how much to confide in Dani, although something deeply internal told me she was okay.

If Dani knew I had another agenda, she didn't press. "Okay, the Sorbonne is in the Latin Quarter. It's on the Left Bank in the fifth, and we're on the Right, in the sixteenth, so you—"

"The fifth?"

Dani caught my blank stare. *"Je m'excuse!* Sorry, Cher, I forgot—you only just got here. How *stupide* of me!" She then began to explain about *arrondissements,* how Paris was divided into different neighborhoods, like Bel Air and Beverly Hills. From what she was saying, I figured that we were like on the right side, in Brentwood, while the Sorbonne—and Josh—was maybe in like West Holly-wood, which appeared to have its own Latino quarter. Or something. Not real close.

"Dani! Cher! *A table!* Dinner's ready—come on." Aunt Lois's melodic voice wafted into the room, bringing our little geography lesson to a close.

The dining room was gargantuan. One wall was all windows. De, Tai, and I looked down at the wide streets of the city below. It was all lit up. "There's the Arch of Triumph!" Tai, excited to have actually recognized some-thing, was wildly pointing to what looked like a chubby upside-down U off in the distance. I followed her bounc-ing finger with my gaze. From this angle, it resembled the center of a Porsche tire, with all these spokes—roads—leading out in different directions away from it. One of which would lead me to Josh.

"The City of Lights—*c'est* mag-nee-feek, *non?*" De was beside me, practicing her French. "Way magnifique," I agreed.

Aunt Lois had gone to enormous lengths to make us feel at home. She'd had the cook prepare a generic American meal: hot dogs and hamburgers. The only French touch were the fries. When Tai pointed this out, Aunt Lois laughed, "French fries are an American inven-tion. Here they're called *pommes frites.*"

David, who'd had to be lured to the table from his

Nintendo game, piped up that he loved *"les burgers royales avec* fries" at Le McDonald's.

By whatever name, they weren't about to be ingested by me or De. Ditto for the grease-spewing hot dogs and burgers. We pleaded exhaustion, while Tai saved our manners by playing the gracious guest. She ate enough for all three of us, including the cheese course at the end. Remind me not to let Daddy come here.

*"Alors,* do you know the important sights you must see?" Uncle Robert started the conversational ball rolling, ticking off not-to-be-missed Parisian monuments, historical churches, and other cultural icons. De listened for the words *haute couture* but, when they didn't come, zoned out. Tai and I put on polite faces. Dani rolled her eyes and rescued us. "Papa? I think I can help direct them—why don't you leave it to me?"

"But you have school this week, Dani. We are thrilled that Cher *et ses amies* are here, but you have exams, and you can't miss them."

Dani didn't miss a beat. *"Bonjour?* When have I *ever* skipped school, Papa? You know me better than that!"

It turned out that, like me, my cousin was a hypercompetent academic type. I don't know why, but I felt proud. She also knew exactly what we wanted. After dinner all four of us squeezed into Dani's room. We sat cross-legged on the shag, gratefully digging into a bowl of juicy grapes Dani had snagged from the kitchen. My cousin then dug out a map and spread it out in front of us.

"First off, where are the cool malls?" De said, wasting no time with preliminaries. She hunched over the map with Dani.

"Malls? Well, we do have Forum des Halles, but most of my friends don't go there. It has the fast food places and the types of shops . . . *alors,* well, we wouldn't actually buy anything there."

Tai and I looked at each other in genuine horror. "But I thought . . . the Galleria? Isn't that a French name?" Tai asked.

Dani was thoughtful. "Galleries Lafayette has pretty much everything. That's a department store, and it's over here, in the ninth. But I didn't think you came here for the department stores—I assumed you wanted the couture houses, *non?*"

Not *non.* Definitely, *mais oui!* Dani then patiently pointed out on the map all the hot couture houses.

Thinking Dani's own wardrobe could use a shot of Chanel, I said, "You really won't be able to come with us?"

*"Malheureusement*—unfortunately—I can't. I am preparing for the *bac,* the baccalaureate—a very important examination that can determine your future."

I didn't grasp all of what Dani was saying, but in my heart I knew that she would pass—and with flying colors. After all, she's related to me.

"But . . ." Dani continued and looked meaningfully from me to De to Tai. *"Tous mes amis* want to meet you. It's, how would you say, *major,* that you're here. So, we've planned *une boum,* a party, for tomorrow night. It will only be a short one because on a school night, the noise must stop at twenty-two hours, but we couldn't wait until the weekend. Everyone wants to welcome you."

"That's so righteous." Tai, sincerely touched, spoke first. "We're totally psyched. Right?" She looked from De to me. I arched my eyebrows. I had like other plans for tomorrow and every other night in France: my search-and-surprise-Josh mission. And a party that lasted twenty-two hours? That was their idea of short? But now that I was actually here, how could I bail and be rude to my cousin? I had a really good feeling about Dani. Maybe we wouldn't stay at the party the whole time.

I bounced back to my most mannerly. "Of course we'd love to come, Dani. What's the dress code?"

"Casual—and it's at Françoise's house. She is my best friend," Dani added, beaming.

Later, when De and Tai went back to their room, Dani pulled out a twin bed from beneath hers, and we got ready to sack out. I was mass ragged. Dani couldn't hide the fatigue vibe either. We were furiously brushing our long, lustrous hair—we did it almost the same way—when Dani flipped her head up and asked, "Do you have a beau, Cher?"

"A bow?" Surprised—like who would wear bows?—I said, "No, um, I usually don't accessorize my hair."

Dani giggled. "No, I mean a boyfriend. Are you seeing someone special?"

I nodded. "You?" Dani's eyes danced, and her face went all moony. She stopped brushing midair and said dreamily, "His name is Claude, and he's . . . well, he's really special."

"Describe," I prompted.

"Okay—he's from the *seizième,* like me," Dani began, then rewound the tape, aware she'd lost me already.

"What I mean is, he's from the same type of background—he lives here, in the sixteenth arrondissement. It's a *très bonne adresse,* Cher, you see?"

"It's way elaborate," I agreed approvingly, not really sure what that had to do with Claude.

"This is important here, to have a boyfriend who is similar to you," Dani added, as if defending her reasoning. "Claude and I are BCBG—it means *bon chic, bon genre*. Our fathers are both established in business. So it's like we share a way of life, can you see?"

I flashed on that miserable night when Elton said he couldn't possibly go out with Tai because, after all, didn't I know who his father was? I wondered if my petite cousin was a snob. But when I looked into her eyes, she was all innocence and sincerity.

"So what does he look like?" I cut to the chase.

"Hot!" She burst out laughing. "That's what you'd say, right? He's very tall, and *très* muscular. Claude never misses a day at the gym."

"Sounds like a certifiable Baldwin," I acknowledged.

"A Baldwin?" Now it was Dani's turn to wander lost in the world of idioms.

"Okay, a Baldwin is what we call a really gorgeous guy—and the girls are Bettys," I explained.

Dani's face lit up in recognition. *"Mais oui!* Here we call them Belmondos, and you are right, Claude is *absolument* a Belmondo. And here, the . . . what did you say, Bettys? We are Veroniques." Dani looked adorably embarrassed. "I'm a Veronique," she said quietly. "Am I right that you are a Betty, cousine Cher?"

"Full-on," I agreed. That's when it hit me. Tai's stepdad-to-be had nailed it. We really *are* a global village after all.

"So your boyfriend?" Dani was now all racing curiosity. "What does he look like—a Baldwin?"

Something told me it was okay to confide all in Dani. I

got up, pulled out the laptop, and divulged Josh's and my entire romantic epic.

Dani was hugely impressed. "And you're e-mailing him now, so he'll still think you're in California? Oh, Cher, that is *très* romantic! I will help you with your surprise. Don't worry about a thing."

I was right about Dani—she was totally cool.

# Chapter 7

*B*onjour, Cher. Time to rise and shine!" Aunt Lois was standing in the doorway of Dani's room. She was wearing a broad smile and a chic figure-flattering Cardin skirt and sweater, accessorized with a Hermès scarf. I looked at the clock next to the bed. Already nine o'clock. Anticipating my question, she said, "Both David and Dani left for school a little while ago. They didn't want to wake you. But your friends are already eating breakfast—come on, there's a phone call for you."

It was Daddy, just checking that we'd gotten in safely. His overprotective vibe has been in major overdrive ever since New York. In my most reassuring tone, I told him we were fine and reminded him about the vitamins and the chiropractor appointment.

I wasn't the only recipient of word from home. Murray-the-possessive had sent an apologetic fax to De, detailing the shame spiral he'd been on since their last fight. "Isn't he sweet?" De soared into the higher digits on the mush-o-meter. "He felt so bad about our last night together, he can't stop thinking of me. He's begging me to call him and tell him he's forgiven."

"You're not going to, are you?" I asked, alarmed. "It's always a good idea to keep boyfriends off balance, especially long-term boyfriends, who might start taking you for granted. It helps to remind them that you've got better things to do than pine for them."

"Hmm, you're right. I'll make him wait a day. I'll do it tomorrow."

*Le petit déjeuner,* as they call it, was served in the sun-washed breakfast room. Aunt Lois's chef laid out a spread for us that rivaled last night's grease-gala, only now it was *de beurre*—I couldn't believe it *was* butter—and *beaucoup* of it. We passed on the croissants and the *pain au chocolat* but gratefully dived into the fruit tarts. Okay, like I know the tart part wasn't exactly good for us, but at least there was fruit. Plus, we were ravenously hungry. If this is how they eat all the time, it's a miracle Aunt Lois is only a slight heifer. And Dani, well, she must have inherited the same buff genes as me and my mom.

Aunt Lois graciously asked if we needed help planning our day, but we assured her that Dani had totally pointed us in the right direction—in a straight line toward the designer showcases. Briefly, I *had* considered going to the Sorbonne first to find Josh, but, okay, so I got a little distracted. I'd find Josh later in the afternoon—and maybe have snagged something even more brutally hot to wear.

"The designers—they're very expensive," Aunt Lois warned. "The price tags may shock you, and the rudeness of the salespeople may put you off."

"We can deal, Aunt Lois. Besides, plastic is like the universal language, right?" I was in a totally optimistic mood.

Aunt Lois shook her head slowly. Snap! I déjà-vued to one of my recurring dreams, the one where I'm telling Mom about my life and she does the same thing as Aunt Lois just did. Chills up my spine: bizarro moment! *"Bonne chance,"* she whispered. "Call if you have any problems."

"Taxi!" We'd been standing outside Dani's building for like ten minutes already. A parade of taxis had totally whizzed by us, as if we were like invisible! Maybe that's what they mean when they say Parisians hate Americans. But how would they even know our nationality?

Just then a stylishly attired middle-aged man walking a huge Labrador came by. "You must be Americans," he said derisively. "May I give you a tip? One doesn't hail taxis in Paris. They won't often stop in the middle of the street." At that, his Labrador started to do its business— right in the street. Nasty!

"Then how do we get to Avenue Mon-tay-nya?" Tai tried significantly to repeat it the way Dani had said it.

The man looked at her like she'd just stepped off the spaceship. "But of course—it's haute couture you girls are after. Well, I suggest the *métro,*" he said, and pointed down the block.

The metro? Isn't that like the subway? As if!

"Thanks for the tip, but we don't do subways," De, not yet completely recovered from our New York underground excursion, informed him. She resumed waving her arm frantically as more cabs passed by.

"Well, there's a taxi station a few blocks away, but there are long lines at this hour. However, if you're going to *do*"—he imitated De's accent—"Paris, the *métro* is the way to *do*"—there it was again—"it." With that, he walked away. I noticed he did not clean up after the dog.

Fifteen minutes later, when we descended the steps under the brightly colored Metropolitain sign, I had to remind myself why we were doing this. Hordes of random humanity pushed past us brusquely as we tried to acclimate. Being in the Paris metro at this hour was a full-contact sport. I got knocked into once by a snazzy Louis Vuitton and again by a Gucci.

An authentic relic from the Mesozoic era, steel-wool hair encased in a bun and enough lines in her face to paint every freeway in L.A., frowned and demanded, *"Combien de billets?"* When we didn't answer instantly, she snarled, *"Première classe? Deuxième classe? Un carnet?"*

I pushed De to the forefront. "Tell her we want three tickets."

"Too-wah bee-yay." De flashed an amazing smile, totally psyched at her ability to communicate. The feeling quickly evaporated, as the artifact glared and rapid-fired back in French so fast, like it would make her day to humiliate us. She totally did not appreciate our attempt to communicate.

Neither did the long line of people behind us. They were rampantly impatient, and even started shouting something at us like, *"Dépêchez-vous!"* I didn't understand what that rock group Depeche Mode had to do with anything. Totally buggin' at their rudeness, I turned around and tried to remind them of their manners. "Hello? Like we're totally new here? Strangers in a strange land?" I'm not sure where I got that from, but it sounded way profound. "Where is your generosity of spirit, your kindness to foreigners, your—"

For my efforts, I was brutally rebuffed and shouted down. Then this incredible Baldwin . . . I mean, Belmondo . . . stepped out of the line and came to our rescue. In perfect English, he said, "Tell me what you need, and I'll get it for you."

He translated quickly and even directed us to the right train. "Don't forget," he said, flashing a killer smile, "get off at Etoile and change for the number one line in the direction of Château de Vincennes. Then take that to the Franklin Roosevelt stop and you will be at your destination." We were majorly grateful and thanked him profusely.

The metro was thankfully way cleaner than the New York subway. And the generics looked a lot less threatening. De and Tai were buried in their respective guidebooks. Only I remembered that we were ambassadors of American youth culture and put my best Maud Frizon forward. I smiled a lot, displaying mass courtesy to my fellow . . . what? Commuters? Had I become a commuter? I noticed a troika of mentally challenged, leather-jacket types eyeing us.

Suddenly, De looked up. "Okay, we're coming to Etoile." The train pulled in to the station and screeched to a stop. Remind me next time—if there is a next time—to wear earplugs. Nothing happened. We waited patiently. To our horror, the train lurched forward and pulled out of the station. What? We couldn't believe it—another example of Parisian rudeness? They didn't bother opening the doors of the train. All polite facade disintegrated, and we started banging on the doors and yelling, "Stop! Stop! We're getting off." The three leather jackets had the nerve to laugh, but mostly people didn't even look up from their newspapers. Finally, a passenger took pity on us. Shaking his head at our ineptitude, he looked up from his paperback and said in fractured English, "Ze doors don't open automatically. You have to open zem yourself if you want to get off." As Tai put it, *"Quel umbelievableness!"*

Several metros later we emerged into the glaring sunlight of the Avenue Montaigne. We blinked. Mecca, in all its glory, was laid out before us. De fell into a trance and started reciting an actual litany until she was out of breath. "Ungaro, Mugler, Courrèges, Armani, Lacroix, Chanel, Hermès, Versace—they're all here, Cher." We were about to cross the threshold into our first Parisian house of haute couture. It was way spiritual.

We opened the first door and were instantly transported into what seemed like a world of egg-shaped hollows. The women's boutique at Ungaro was all luminous backdrop highlighting a rich palette of colors. De started to hyperventilate.

*"Bonjour, mesdemoiselles."* An icy voice brought us back to planet earth. It belonged to a stiffly attired saleswoman, wearing a wide belt cinched within an inch of her life. It probably accounted for her miserable nature. She advanced toward us and gave us the once-over.

De pulled herself together quickly. "We've come to look at the new collection," she said, repeating verbatim the guidebook's advice on what to say.

"The new collection?" The saleswoman arched her

severely drawn eyebrows. "I'm sorry to inform you the collection is not new anymore. It was new four months ago." She was about to spew more venom when she got distracted by Tai, who was innocently fingering a dress. "Mademoiselle! One does not touch the merchandise here!"

Rebuffed but too clueless to be rebuked, Tai blinked and innocently asked, "Then how do I look at it?"

"If you desire something, it will be brought out to you," the saleswoman said sternly. It looked as if power shopping was out. We began to detail our hearts' desires.

"That silk blouse over there." I pointed out a classic that would go spectacularly well with my Chanel suit. "Does that come in a size six?"

She eyeballed me and announced sharply, "You would be a thirty-six in that blouse, mademoiselle."

Thirty-six? Not even! Then I remembered that European sizing *is* different. Still, I hate to say it—I feel like a Forgotten Woman or something.

Okay, so our shopping odyssey had gotten off to a slightly rocky start, but as we gained valuable experience in the French mode, I'm proud to say we scaled the mountain and emerged victorious. We hit only the best houses and, with each, made fewer and fewer gaffes.

Chanel was everything we dreamed it would be, down to the doorknobs. They were shaped like crystal perfume bottle-stoppers. The displays surprised us: lots of leather and chains instead of the fitted suits like in L.A., but that only encouraged De to whip out her credit cards. She snared a fierce leather vest and velvet jeans.

Tai lost it at Courrèges. When she found out *Soldes* didn't mean "sold out" but "on sale," she picked up a totally '60s pair of retro hip-hugging bell bottoms. Like it wouldn't be my style? But I had to admit, if any Betty could carry it off, it was Tai. With a midriff-tied shirt, at least she could, as Josh would say, continue to explore the exciting world of bare midriffs.

Josh! Shopping had almost completely distracted me from my mission. I looked at my watch. Plenty of time to get to the Sorbonne. Which I was just about to suggest, when De and Tai cut in on my thought process.

"I don't know about you, but I could use some refreshment right about now," Tai announced, adding unnecessarily that her stomach was rumbling.

"Caffeine-laced French vanilla latte sounds like heaven," De agreed.

"Let's see if we can find a California Pizza Kitchen," Tai suggested.

"CPK? Tscha! We're in France. Let's find some awesomely Parisian outdoor café." De scanned the street. "How about over there?" She pointed to an outdoor café, with umbrellas that said Tabac on them.

A few minutes later, we were gratefully settled at a table, our shopping bags at our way tired feet. We tried to make sense of the menu.

"Garçon!" De shouted. "I've always wanted to say that." She looked at us and giggled. No garçons, garçonettes, or waiters of any type heeded the call, however. We waited. I was already learning something. The Parisians were way laid back as a species. And manners were definitely not a strong suit.

Finally, a totally doable waiter with rippling muscles came to take our order. He was all Antonio Banderas, except French instead of Spanish.

De began. "Je voo-dray une petite salade neece-wahs. Pas de oil, pas de beurre, pas de foie. Le dressing avec balsamic vinegar. Et un café latte, French vanilla." De finished jubilantly, glowing with competence.

In perfect English, the waiter read it back to her. "So I take it, mademoiselle, you want to order a few lettuce leaves and a dry hunk of tuna, nothing on it."

De was about to make verbal toast of him when out of nowhere a flock of pigeons dive-bombed into our personal space. "Eeeww! Nasty!" I jumped up and grabbed my shopping bags. "We are *so* Audi! Come on!"

The waiter found this was wildly amusing. "If you cannot take a few pigeons, mesdemoiselles," he managed between coughs of laughter, "I suggest you return home *immédiatement*. Here, you will find, even in the chicest streets, pigeons are quite plentiful. It's part of the charm of Paris."

We felt insulted, but in the end hunger won out and we stayed. Tai ordered a quiche Lorraine. "I have no idea what it is, but it sounds French," she said, delighted with herself.

Feeling guilty about this morning's tart-indiscretion, I decided to play it safe so I ordered an entire plate—only here they call it a *plateau*—of fruit. I pictured this pyramid of succulent fresh fruit. So when the waiter brought over this like crustacean convention—mussels, oysters, and clams—it took every ounce of my well-bred manners not to go ballistic.

"There must be some mistake." I smiled and started, all polite. "I asked for fruit—not this."

"No, mademoiselle, you did not." He looked me straight in the eye. "This is what you ordered."

I picked up the menu and pointed. "No, *this* is what I asked for, a plateau of fruit—you know, strawberries, cantaloupe, oranges—see, it's the same in any language."

"I'm afraid it is far from the same," he gloated, sounding not the least bit afraid, or, hello? even apologetic. *Un plateau des fruits de mer* is seafood."

I turned to De. "It is? What's fruit got to do with clams? And why didn't you warn me?"

She shrugged. "I'm only in French Two, Cher, we didn't get to invertebrates yet." With that, she dug into her salad.

"Perhaps you should come to Paris a little more prepared next time, eh?" The waiter smirked and turned on his heel, disappearing into the café before I could get a zinger in.

"What am I supposed to do with this?" I whined.

"Don't pop an artery, Cher, just eat it." De, in her least sympathetic mode, never even looked up from her tuna.

"Whatever." I was totally fed up but woefully hungry. I grimaced but allowed the oysters to slide down my throat.

"Where to now?" Tai asked, wiping the butter off her face with a napkin. "More shopping?"

"Not for me," I answered. "The little gold tick-tock around my wrist informs me that it's time to embark on my mission. I'm going to find the Sorbonne, but if you guys don't want to come, that's cool."

"No way, Cher. We're not letting you wander around by yourself. May I remind you that I'm the only one who speaks French?" De looked serious. My eyebrows shot up. "Okay, well, at least a little better than you do. Anyway, when you find Josh, we'll be Audi, but until you do, the name of this tune is Unity."

\* \* \*

The area around the Sorbonne was totally different from the one we'd just been at. Instead of designer boutiques, it was riddled with art galleries, cafés, and used bookstores. It seemed like a way literary nabe. No grand boulevards, either, just a bunch of crammed-together cobblestone streets. I hoped the taxi driver wasn't dropping us here—my platforms on cobblestones?

*"Alors,* we are here." The cabbie stopped at a corner. The street sign said, Plâce de la Sorbonne. I pulled out some francs and let him take the right amount. "Don't forget a tip," I said generously. The cab driver looked astounded and grabbed a few more bills.

"I think you might have overpaid," Tai said.

"Whatever." I flashed a W and looked around. I felt a wave of anticipation. So this is where Josh is. I looked up at the huge building facing us. The words *Liberté, Egalité, Fraternité* were carved in marble over the door. Cool— we're in totally the right place. Like at home Josh belonged to Sigma Delta Pi, but maybe he joined *Liberté, Egalité* here.

Inside, it didn't resemble any frat house I'd ever seen. Like where were the beer cans? The loud music? It was more like my school, with classrooms. We walked down a huge hallway, until we found an office and someone to ask.

We were greeted—actually, ignored—by a matronly-looking heifer who refused to look up from her . . . what was that machine anyway? I think I remember from like the Jurassic era—a typewriter?

"Excuse me," I finally ventured. "Avez-voos parlay English?"

"Clearly, mademoiselle, I parlay it better than you do

French," she growled without even looking up. Was "rude" their national language?

I decided to let it go. "Good. I'm looking for a student." I gave her Josh's name. "He's in the work-study program here at the Sorbonne. It's way urgent," I added importantly, "and I think he might be in this fraternity. Can you tell me what room he's in?"

She finally deigned to look at us. "Fraternity? Mademoiselle, just because he studies here does not mean he lives here. This is an academic building, not a fraternity. No one resides here."

"But . . ." That nervous feeling in my stomach was starting up.

"Clearly, you have arrived to look for him with not enough information. What is his address?"

"Josh's address? It's here." The only place I'd ever FedEx'ed packages to was the Sorbonne. I just assumed . . .

She let out a huge sigh and said, "I take it he is an American like you?"

"Duh, of course!" I said enthusiastically.

"There are many American work-study students here. If you wait, I will look up his name." With great effort, she hoisted herself out of the chair and disappeared into a back office. She emerged a few minutes later, holding a file and waving it at me. "The boy you are looking for? His residence hall is Les Etats-Unis."

I practically curtsied. "Can you point out which building that is?"

She narrowed her eyes and snapped, "You don't see the residence hall from here. It is in Cité Universitaire—in the fourteenth. Pas ici."

I turned to De, who explained, "It's not around here.

She's saying it's fourteen blocks—or maybe miles, I'm not sure—from here."

"How do we get to it?" I went for helpless again.

"I suggest *le métro*," she said, and, dismissing us, pointed out the door.

Back to the metro? De, Tai, and I looked at each other. Not even. One transportation fiasco a day was enough.

The taxi ride to Cité Universitaire took way longer than the one to the Sorbonne. The cab driver took more francs, too. A nervous feeling totally engulfed me. We were almost here, the destination I'd been dreaming about. But what now? What if I didn't find Josh? What if I did? I was flailing in a sea of confused feelings.

Pull yourself together, Cher, I told myself. It's Josh. And he needs you. He'll be furiously glad to see you. It'll be perfect. And when the driver stopped in front of an actual campus—okay, it wasn't a real campus like UCLA, but at least it wasn't just a building on a street—I felt better.

Still, my heart was furiously pounding as we crossed the campus and walked up the steps of the building marked Etats-Unis. De and Tai followed close behind.

A goofy-looking student with an overbite and a chia-goatee was behind the control desk. "Umm, hi," I ventured.

*"Bonjour,"* he answered, and followed up with something that sounded all pushed together, like pwis-ja-voos a-day?

A sense of overwhelming frustration suddenly gripped me. "Doesn't anybody speak American around here?"

"Don't wig out, girlfriend, I can do this," De said. With that, she calmly turned to the doofus behind the desk and charmingly explained why we were here. Despite the debacle at lunch, De totally made herself understood and even seemed to get what the geek was rambling and gesturing on about. If I didn't know De better, I'd think she was flirting.

She turned to me. "Translation: he says his name is Pierre."

Before I could interject that like I *care* what his name is, De continued. "And he knows that Josh's group is out on a field trip." De turned back to Pierre and gave him a devastating smile—she *was* flirting! "The group won't be back until the day after tomorrow, but Pierre wants to know if you want to leave a message for him."

My stomach sank. Josh was away? I'd be missing two whole days that I could be spending with him. Serious bummer time. "Tell him I said thanks, but no thanks. I want to surprise Josh, so tell him not to say we were here."

I was buggin'. No one spoke American, people were rude, fruit was oysters, pigeons were considered charming lunch company, and worst of all, Josh wasn't even here. Well, not right here, right now. Which was where I needed him to be. Daddy was right. We really *were* in a foreign country.

A party was like the last thing on my wish list, but when we got back, Dani was so up for it, I couldn't beg off and disappoint her. She was all bubbly about what she was going to wear and all her friends who were— according to her—dying to meet us. "They can't wait to practice their English on you." Dani said this as if it were a good thing. "They all made an agreement—no one will speak French tonight, *seulement anglais*."

"Cool," I said, applying jet black, lash-lengthening mascara and thinking, just what I need, to spend the night listening to fractured English and pretending to like care. But then I stopped myself. What am I doing? It was as if all the bad manners I'd been exposed to today were totally rubbing off on me. I was better than that, I was stronger than that.

# Chapter 8

**D**ani's friend Françoise lived in a high-rise that was identical to Dani's. But when Françoise opened the door, it was another world. Make that another century. Maybe it was just for the party, but it was all "return with us to *Saturday Night Fever*." I half expected Tony Manero to come gliding out in his white suit. There was an actual disco ball suspended from the ceiling, and the furniture had obviously been pushed back against the walls to create what passed for a dance floor. Coffee tables were scattered about and riddled with chips and dips. And it looked as if the entire party was in one room.

Françoise herself was all blushy and giggly as she shook our hands way too vigorously. Why did it not surprise me that she spoke in exclamation points? *"Bonsoir!* Welcome! I am Françoise—it's so . . . cool"—she accented it the same way Dani did—"that you have come!" Before I could even slip into polite mode, her face swerved in dangerously close to mine but no actual contact was made. The French version of an air kiss, I guessed.

*"Nos amies—je m'excuse, seulement anglais ce soir—*I mean our friends are so want to meet you!"

And so they are did! Just as Françoise yelled out, "Everyone—here they are! It is Cher and Dionne and Tai!" a horde of random Parisian preppies completely invaded our personal space, all yapping, shaking hands, and doing that faux-kiss thing at the same time.

We were barraged with introductions followed by questions. "Do you go to the beach every day? Do you surf? Do you know any movie stars?" The boys were all, "Do you know where Pamela Anderson lives? Do you know the Red Hot Cheeli Peepers? Do you know Dylan and Brenda? Is Kelly going to get together with Brandon?"

From what Dani had said, I assumed these kids were smart, but hello? Like they got that *Baywatch* was fiction but thought *90210* was real? And besides, they were three years behind. Maybe it's a time-zone thing.

What they lost in the battle of fact vs. fiction, they totally got on the fashion front. Dani's friends did have style. Among the usual mix of micro Armanis, backless halter dresses, and Versace sheaths, I spotted at least one flaming red Lacroix and a thigh-high beaded number by Jacques Azagury and several Muglers.

Only the boys lacked daring in their duds. Polos and khakis seemed to be the uniform, with a retro *Miami Vice* look jarringly thrown in here and there.

De and Tai were still hopelessly stuck in the crowd when Dani grabbed my elbow and pulled me away. *"Pardon, pardon,"* she said, guiding me through the crowd and toward the couch. On it sat a Baldwin of the most major proportions. He was all thick black moussed hair, chiseled jaw, burning blue eyes, at this moment clouded by the smoke from his lit cigarette. I noticed a few burn marks and crushed butts on the sofa.

"This is Claude," Dani said in a low reverential tone. Claude didn't uncross his legs or get up. He motioned for me and Dani to sit down. Unlike the other boys, he wore a button-down Hugo Boss shirt—way down, so a forest of chest hair (totally *not* my style) was exposed. One overdeveloped arm rested lazily on the back of the sofa. Claude had rolled his short-sleeves up so there'd be no mistaking we'd entered muscle beach. The survey said: Jordan Catalano on steroids.

"So you are ze famous Cher" were the first words out of his mouth—which, not to pass judgment, was not the instantly kissable kind. Thin lips. And the way he said Cher, rolling the *r,* sounded almost like a taunt, but I decided not to jump to hasty conclusions. This was the boy Dani was rampantly sprung on.

I made all light and breezy. "Yes, I'm the famous Cher," I agreed, flipping my hair back, "and it's my pleasure to meet the famous Claude!" Uh-oh, speaking in exclamations was catchy.

"So what do you think of Paris so far, eh?" He made it sound like a challenge. Ignoring his tone of voice, I started to tick off all the fun we'd had today. I even tried to make a joke about my cultural cluelessness. "Imagine thinking *fruits de mer* was fruit!" I laughed a little too hard. So did Dani. But Claude didn't. He just stared and blew smoke, not exactly *at* me but close enough to make my eyes sting. Concern about my eyeliner overshadowed any personal offense I might have taken.

Gamely, I tried another conversational route. "So how

did you guys meet? At school or something?" When Claude didn't answer, Dani jumped in. "It was at Françoise's *rallie.*"

"Like a pep rally?" I asked. "We have them at school."

Dani looked confused, "No, not pep. Here, a *rallie* is a special kind of party"—she surveyed the room—"not like this one, but one where it is suggested . . . I mean, assumed . . . that, how do I say this? That Veroniques will meet Belmondos. *Comprends-tu?*"

"You mean like arranged dates or something?"

"Not exactly. Just that you meet the right kind of boy or girl, of a similar background. Make a good catch," Dani explained, looking adoringly over at her own personal catch, Claude. Who, I noticed, had not made a move to put his arm around her or do any kind of PDA—public display of affection.

I was about to comment on how retro-snobby rallies sounded when just then someone cranked the music up loudly. As if on cue, the crowd interrogating De and Tai broke away and hit the dance floor. Claude got up, too. Without a word to either of us, he disappeared into the crowd.

"So what do you think of him?" Dani pounced the second Claude was out of hearing range. "You are my cousin, and you must give me your true opinion."

"Baldwin to the max," I said with as much admiration as I could muster. "Strong, silent type, too, huh?"

"Oh, he has his moments." Dani giggled and then got all serious. "Claude likes to take people in, before he feels comfortable enough to open up with them. That's his way. A little shy at first."

Shy? Like it wasn't the first descriptive I would've pinned on Claude.

"Well, I'd better check on De and Tai," I said, hoping to short-circuit the Claude talk. I started to get up when Dani grabbed my arm and directed my attention to an underlit corner of the room directly across from us. There stood two exquisitely dressed people, apparently deep in conversation. He was wearing a black leather jacket; she was in . . . wait a minute, that's what De wore tonight. Duh! It *was* De! And the leather jacket standing way too close to her? Classic: in the total Gallic godlike sense of the word.

Even from where I was sitting I could tell he was all bronze, brawny, and staring at her with an intentness boys usually reserve for Monday night football. I couldn't take my eyes off them. He said something, and De let out a throaty laugh—and it was real, not the kind of phony one when you're trying to make the boy think he's really funny, even though what he said was totally lame.

Dani watched me watching them. "I see your friend De has met André."

"And André would be . . . ?" I asked, still spying on De.

"Just the biggest catch in our crowd! He is *très* popular, *très* intelligent—at the top of the class. And *très* rich. But he has a bit of the rebel in him. He rides a motorcycle and has a tattoo. Girls have been trying to land him for years, but so far no one can seem to pin him down."

"Afraid of the C-word, huh?"

"The C-word?" Dani asked. "I'm not sure what you mean."

"Commitment. Like he's afraid to commit. Boys are way famous for that. It's the same all over the world," I explained, feeling very global.

"Maybe, but as long as I have known him, I have never seen André look at any girl the way he looks at Dionne."

71

I didn't get a chance to digest that tidbit because just then someone turned the music up ruthlessly loud. The wall-to-wall kids on the dance floor made for the couches and love seats. Clearly, they knew what was coming. So did Dani.

"Here she comes," Dani said snidely, "the one embarrassment to our group, Monique. She always has to show off at every party."

Show-off was a rampantly lame description for Monique. She had a body that, in boy talk, wouldn't quit. Sheathed in a skintight, low-cut Alaïa and what had to be a Wonderbra, Monique danced with tsunamic ferocity. All by herself. No boy in the room dared to try to keep up with her. To the frenetic beat, she was like a blender set on pulverize. Amazingly, her limbs did not detach from their sockets as she flung them about.

Which of course reminded me of Josh. I mean, the way Monique danced, so bizarrely disjointed? Not that Josh resembles her, but he's so adorable when he tries to keep a beat.

"She'd do anything to get Claude from me," Dani said.

"Tscha! Dani, she's got so totally nothing on you." I snapped to and tried to reassure my cousin. "Duh, she's like a total Monet."

Before Dani could ask, I explained that a Monet is someone who looks great at a distance but up close is a mess. Dani giggled and said, "Here we call them Picassos—from a distance, a pretty picture, but all scrambled up close."

Monique was still flinging away wildly, practically frothing at the mouth. All the boys in the room were into serious overdrool, and all eyes, including Claude's, were glued to her every gravity-defying gyration.

Except for one pair of eyes, that is. Okay, so they were partially hidden behind glasses, but even so, I could see they were on . . . no, not me—hmm, that's surprising— but on Dani. And the look on his face was pure adoration. For this boy, Monique didn't exist. He seemed muscularly challenged, but his clothes were so loose and baggy it was hard to tell.

I nudged Dani and stage-whispered, "Who's that?"

She tore her eyes away from Monique and refocused to meet my field of vision. "Who? Jean-Michel?" she said distractedly.

"He's kind of cute," I said. "And"—I thought maybe I was delivering a news flash—"he's been staring at you in *that* way."

Dani politely rebuffed me and turned back to Monique. "No, you must be mistaken, Cher. Jean-Michel is one of my oldest friends. Why would he stare at me in any way?"

When the record ended, Dani turned to me and said, "In all my excitement about the party I forgot to ask you—did you find the Sorbonne?" I explained that we'd made it as far as Josh's dorm, but it would be at least two days until he returned from his field trip. Dani was righteously sympathetic.

I wondered why Claude hadn't asked her to dance and starting scanning the room for him. Instead, I saw De and André dancing to the strains of "When a Man Loves a Woman." It seemed like André's arms were wrapped around her awfully tightly, but maybe that was just the dance style here.

"Hmm, I wonder if it hasn't finally happened." That was Dani, musing.

"If what hasn't finally happened?"

"What you would call love at first sight—between

André and De. This looks like the real thing. And not only for André. De looks pretty involved."

"Not even! Dani, did I mention that De has a boyfriend? She's totally in love with Murray. I had to practically drag her away from him to even get her to come with me. I mean, De can flirt, but she . . ."

Dani finished my sentence. "Can't fall in love with another? I don't know Cher. I have never seen André act like this before. Usually, he'll make polite conversation and charm many girls, but by now? He'd be . . ."

"Audi?" This time I finished for her. She got the gist.

This was all too weird. I needed to get to De. But it suddenly occurred to me that, like, wait, where was Tai? I hadn't seen her in a while. And then I heard this mass giggling and saw pointing coming from the other side of the room. I looked to see what the commotion was about. Instantly, I flashed back to other commotions at other parties—and my worst fears were confirmed. It *was* Tai. Only this time, thankfully, it looked as if the bumps and bruises were only going to be psychic.

Tai must have gone to the bathroom. When she came out, there was, like, this trail of toilet paper stuck to her heel. Which Dani's friends found rampantly hysterical—but then again, aren't these the people who still think Jerry Lewis is a laugh riot?

As usual, Tai was clueless. She had no idea everyone was laughing ferociously at her, and pointing behind her back. Trying desperately to get it, she was actually laughing, too. I jumped up off the couch and made for her, but someone beat me to it. It was Jean-Michel. He'd sprung up and torn over to her. He put his arm around her and carefully led her out of the room, far away from the shrieking hyenas. He was totally gallant.

I made my way through the crowd to find them. They were in the kitchen, and Jean-Michel was on his hands and knees, pulling the toilet paper off her shoe. Tai was brutally humiliated but tried to keep it together as she thanked him profusely. She lost it when she saw me.

"Cher," she said, breaking out in huge sobs, "I can't believe I made a fool of myself in front of Dani's friends. I can't go out there and face them again."

I put my arms around her. "Forget it, Tai, everyone has embarrassing moments." I looked hopefully at Jean-Michel. "Right?"

He smiled and his look totally morphed. He had a killer smile. White teeth and dimples to die for. Definite potential. *"Absolument,"* he confirmed. "I remember one time, I was trying to impress this girl with how good I was on Rollerblades? Except I am not much the athlete and have not much grace, either. I tried to do a wheelie and fell plop on my *derrière."*

Tai giggled at his scrambled syntax.

"By the way," he continued, standing up and extending his hand, "I am Jean-Michel, a friend of Dani's."

"I know, she told me," I said, clasping his hand.

"She did?" Jean-Michel seemed surprised that Dani had mentioned him. I didn't have the heart to tell him she was only answering my question.

"Uh-huh, she said you guys go way back."

*"C'est vrai.* We are the oldest of friends."

But you think of her as more than just a friend, is what I wanted to say—but it was way too soon for that. Besides, I had to restore Tai's confidence in herself first. I whipped out a tissue and gently blotted her makeup, which had started to run. Then I pulled out my compact and gave Tai a quick repair.

"Come on, Tai, we're going back out there. I won't allow you to be chased away from the party by a bunch of jerks. Just stay with me and we'll face them together." Tai looked doubtful.

"Thanks, Jean-Michel," I said. "That was a real props you did, and we won't forget it." I couldn't tell, but I think he might have blushed.

My get-back-behind-the-wheel strategy worked. As soon as we reentered party central, a not-half-bad-looking though string-beany dude asked Tai to dance. She glanced at me for approval. I instantly saw that he was sincere and not trying to humiliate her, so I gave it.

I was mentally patting myself on the back for being right about Jean-Michel when I felt real hands on my shoulders. They were working their way in a circular mini-massage movement. "So, Cher, how about a dance?" It was Claude, and he had that kind of leering tone again. I guess he no longer considered me a stranger.

"No, thanks, I don't think so." I spun around so he'd be forced to get his hands off me. "But I bet Dani would like to dance."

"It's not Dani I asked, it's you," he said again, and bored into me with his way intense eyes. A girl could get lost in them. I looked away.

"Look, Claude. I know you're just being gallant, and all"—actually I knew no such thing—"but really, I'm totally fine. I'm having a blast just meeting all Dani's friends and all. This is a pretty cool fiesta."

If Claude realized I was giving him a polite way of backing off, he showed no sign. "This is considered a cool party in California?" he said. "You can't be serious. I can assure you that there are much better parties here in

Paris. And much better clubs. *Alors,* I can show you—
why don't you and I blow this joint?"

I was torn between wanting to believe this was
Claude's way of being polite to a newcomer and the icky
realization that he might be coming on to me. But then
again, maybe the touchy-feely stuff was just the Parisian
way. But the next thing he said blew the lid off ambiguity.

"You know, I could be your private guide to Paris, show
you things you don't find in the guidebooks. I really want
to get to know you *much better.*"

I faced Claude and gave him my most stern. "I'll
pretend I didn't hear that. Now, if you'll excuse me, I've
got friends to find." I turned and did the best stalking-
away move I possibly could in four-and-one-half-inch
heels.

Am I in some alternate universe or something? Claude
is Dani's boyfriend—why would he come on to me?
Okay, I know I'm generally irresistible, but Dani is my
cousin and, hello? she's *in* the room. What's up with him?
And speaking of what's up—zup with De? She still had
not torn herself away from André.

Much later, back at Dani's, I tried to find out.

"So, De, I see you made a new friend?" I tried to be
nonchalant, but De was all defensive. "Don't do that tone
with me, Cher. I came here as a favor to you, remember?
But as long as I *am* here, I might as well make the most of
it."

"And the name of the most would be, if I'm not
mistaken, André, right?"

De looked to see, like, how judgmental was I? She came
down on the side of mostly innocent. She softened.

77

"André. Cute, huh? He's really nice, Cher, and he sincerely wants to help me get a more complete experience of Paris. Nothing wrong with that is there?" Before I could answer, she added, "Tomorrow night he's taking me on a tour."

I thought about Claude's invitation to me. Well, this was different. It's not as if André was somebody else's boyfriend. But speaking of boyfriends, "What about Murray?" I ventured.

"What about him?" De looked annoyed. "It's not like I'm cheating on Murray. I'm just going sightseeing is all. That's the best way to see Paris, with someone who actually lives here. And that's all it is, Cher, so don't have an aneurysm. Besides, I'm calling Murray tomorrow."

"Okay, girlfriend, I'm just wiped. It's been an enlightening day and night."


I was ragged, but I couldn't sleep so I decided to turn on the laptop and check my e-mail. The little beep must have awakened Dani.

"I hope you had a good time tonight, Cher," she said. She flicked on the lamp. "Here, now you can actually see what you are typing."

I smiled at her. Dani was all, "I have to apologize for my *stupide* friends who made fun of Tai."

That was just the opening I needed. "Well, you do have one friend who's totally gallant."

Dani furrowed her brow.

"Jean-Michel. He jumped to Tai's rescue. He even tried to make her feel better by telling her a silly story about falling on his butt when he was trying to impress a girl."

Dani laughed. *"Oui,* I remember that."

Duh! It suddenly hit me—of course, Dani was the girl. Jean-Michel has probably been sprung on her, like, forever.

"So what's the 411 on Jean-Michel? Does he have a girlfriend?" I asked.

"Jean-Michel? No, he's too much into his art for going after girls."

"His art? Is he an actor?" I asked. In California when people say they're into their art, it means they're auditioning for a sitcom.

"No, not an actor. A painter. Jean-Michel is an *artiste*. That has been his passion all his life."

That—and you, I thought. "And you and he are very good friends?"

"The best. After Françoise, Jean-Michel is my closest confidant. I tell him everything, and he tells me."

Somehow, I didn't think Jean-Michel could be completely candid with Dani. Or if he was, she was too blind to see it.

I decided to shelve the boy talk for the moment to focus on the laptop. But there was no mail from Josh—duh, what did I expect, he was away on a field trip. I shut the computer, and Dani turned out the light. She fell asleep right away but not me. My mind was all racing. I had made a valiant attempt at not jumping to conclusions. But I so totally pride myself on personal perceptions and click! there it was again: Claude was rampantly wrong for Dani. If he'd come on to me, who knows how many other . . . um . . . Veroniques he'd cheated on Dani with? Yet Dani didn't see past his proper background and amazing, yet deceitful eyes. Worse, she was adorably clueless about Jean-Michel.

That's when it hit me. I had to gently help Dani take the blinders off. But I didn't have a lot of time to do it. I was in Paris for less than a week. Okay, like, so I know I promised Josh I'd try to curb my natural impulses to help—he keeps reminding me about how they sometimes backfire—but this is different. Dani is family. And she needs me.

# Chapter 9

*T*he next morning Tai got a call from the alterna-kids she'd met on the plane. "They want to hook up with us," she explained after she'd hung up.

As if! "Uh, I don't think so, Tai—after all, we've got a lot of ground to cover."

"I really like them, Cher, and so would you if you gave them a chance. Besides, they want to meet us at a cultural place. And we did say we'd get some culture when we were here, right?"

"What cultural place?" De inquired suspiciously.

"Something called the Pomp-a-doo Center. Christian told us about it, and it's in the guidebook." And when had Tai suddenly become the guidebook diva? She continued, "It's totally important, the most popular modern art museum in the entire world."

De's face lit up. I was about to ask why she was

suddenly so pumped for culture when she sputtered, "The Pompidou Center—that's right by Alaïa!"

Aunt Lois, who'd overheard the last part of our conversations burst out laughing. "Come on, girls, I will help you plan a route for today. It will be your culture day."

Works for me. It's not as if I can see Josh yet anyway. And if I get some culture today, when I do see him tomorrow? I'll be ferociously global.

The Louvre was the first stop on our customized tour. Tai read from the *Pocket Guide to Paris* Christian had stuffed in her backpack. "Okay, so this is like the largest museum in the world," she said as we followed her through an archway into a wide-open quad. "It's two hundred years old."

I didn't immediately see the Louvre but something unexpected instead. "Cool! Look at that." I pointed to a glass pyramid standing straight up in the middle of the square. A long line of people snaked from the door around the courtyard. "They have their own Rock 'n' Roll Hall of Fame! Complete with a gazillion tourists lined up to get in."

"Hello? This is the entrance to the Louvre, Cher—even I know that," De said, rolling her eyes. "Besides, there are no French rock stars."

"You know what?" Tai said, looking up from the guidebook. "The entrance to the Louvre and the Rock 'n' Roll Hall of Fame were designed by the same architect, some I. M. Pei guy. That's why they look alike. Anyone could've confused them."

I felt vindicated.

"I guess we get in line," Tai offered.

Get in line? De and I looked at each other, and thinking about our platform heels, I said, "I don't think so, Tai. Look it up, isn't there some way you can like pay and cut the line?"

Bummer. There wasn't. By the time we actually got inside the Louvre, we were way tired. But then De had this golden idea, and we all brightened. "Let's do this culture thing like shopping. We'll power shop through the important works. It'll be so efficient. Which way to the Mona Lisa, Tai?"

Tai didn't even have to answer. All we had to do was follow the crowd. Still, it seemed like we were walking forever, up a flight of marble steps, down another, through some totally icky mummy room until we finally reached the painting. But like there were so many people crowded around it, we could hardly see anything. "Why don't they just put it in the front?" I suggested helpfully. "It would save a lot of time and more people could see it at once."

"Why don't you put that idea in the suggestion box, Cher?"

De was being snide, but I let it go. "Maybe I will."

And when we finally did get close enough? Mona was more Monet than Betty. She was all flat hair and in totally the wrong colors. She did have this half-smile thing going on. It's like what I do sometimes—affect this modest yet mysterious smile intended to get a boy's attention. So maybe Mona had a thing for Leonardo. Who knew?

"Okay, let's take a picture of us in front of it," I proposed. How cool would *that* be to bring back to Christian? De and I did our best imitation of the Mona smile while Tai snapped away. I couldn't understand why we got such evil stares from the rest of the crowd. It's not like we broke the rules and used a flash. My thinking? If you weren't careful, this Parisian rudeness could really be catchy.

After Mona, we stopped in front of a sculpture that Tai insisted was important, the Venus de Milo. But like, duh, if it was so important, you'd think someone would glue the arms back on.

"Next stop on the culture express?" I asked Tai. I was feeling way good about this day.

"Your aunt suggested Notre-Dame." She flipped the pages to look it up.

"Notre-Dame? I know they have a great football team, but so what? We could see that at home." This time it was De being clueless. "Duh, De, Notre-Dame's totally famous. Don't you remember the Hunchback? Like from Cliff's Notes?" I prompted.

Notre-Dame turned out to be a cathedral on an island in the middle of the river that divides Paris in half. As we crossed over this ancient bridge, I noticed a wide, flat boat filled with tourists taking pictures. Couples were embracing. Naturally, I thought of Josh. "The Bat-oh-Moosh," Tai said, reading. "That's the boat ride down the Seine River."

"Bat-oh-Mousse," I repeated. Maybe Josh and I could do that later.

"Bateau-*Mouche*, Cher, not like hair gel." De was correcting me again.

Mousse, Mouche. Whatever.

At Notre-Dame, we didn't see any hunchbacks or football souvenirs either. On the outside, there were these way cool gargoyles. Inside, the place was like wall-to-wall hordes of random tourists, invading dark musty rooms with stained-glass windows. The colors reminded me somewhat of De's Hanae Mori dress, only brighter.

There was a narrow spiral staircase leading up to a tower. Tai had one foot on the first step. "It says you get a close-up view of the gargoyles." Why this seemed to excite her was beyond me, but 387 steps up to the towers? As if!

Even though we didn't climb up, we did pose for a picture outside the gate. I could feel myself getting more cultural by the moment. Daddy and Christian would be proud.

The Eiffel Tower was next on the list that Aunt Lois had drawn up. As we stood beneath the colossal A-frame, Tai did the let's-get-educated thing. "The Eiffel Tower was erected in 1889 for the World Exhibition. It's 1052 feet tall and weighs 9,700 tons. It's in like fifteen thousand pieces, held together by seven million rivets. You can take the elevator up to the top."

Tai tilted her head way back and looked up. "It says it sways on windy days."

De licked her forefinger and put it in the air. "Winds are from the east-southeast, about thirty miles per hour," she announced in her best Willard Scott.

"I don't know about you," I said to Tai, "but swaying in the wind at the top of this pieced-together monument—like, why didn't they cover it?—I don't see how that results in culture. I mean, my hair will totally be in knots. And your hair, Tai—forget it. Let's do a lap, take a picture, and say that we did it, okay?"

De seconded with a limp-wrsted high-five, but Tai just shrugged her shoulders. Then she realized it was time to meet her new friends at the Pompidou Center, anyway. De and I looked at each other. As usual, we were thinking the same thing. "Uh, that doesn't really leave us time for Alaïa, Tai," De said.

"Well," she said, thinking hard, "you said it was close by, right? Why don't you guys go to Alaïa and I'll go to the Pompidou Center. I'll hang with Bailey, Charisma, and those guys, and then we'll all hook up later?"

"Sounds like a plan to me," De agreed.

But something was bothering me. It took a while until I realized what it was. It was Daddy. He'd made us promise to stick together, and here we were separating already. De and Tai quelled my fears. "We'll only be a few blocks from each other—and we're only separating for like an hour or so." We had the cab drop off Tai first and then De and me at Rue de Moussy—Alaïa street!

And when we got there? All my fears totally evaporated. Azzedine Alaïa was by far the most classic place we'd been to so far. "This is the center of it all," De breathed reverentially. "This is where it begins and ends. You snag a dress here, and it doesn't show up, even in Beverly Hills, for like months."

The selection was gargantuan. We tried on one slinky, body-molding dress after another. We looked incredible in all of them. It was going to be torture to decide. By the time we did, after racking up seven outfits between us, over an hour had elapsed.

"We'd better make serious tracks," I said. "Tai's probably worrying about us."

Right about that. Tai was worrying—in fact, she was hysterical—but it had nothing to do with us being late. We found Tai in a square outside the modern art museum known as the Pompidou Center. And who designed this abomination, I wondered, looking up at this way huge, inside-out structure with the pipes still showing?

"Cher! De!" It was the most high-pitched and fevered Tai I'd ever heard. She was surrounded by people but spotted us and yelled above the clamor. In the square outside the Pompidou Center there were fire-eaters, hypnotists, dancers, acrobats, clowns, and mimes—pointing, shouting, jumping up and down. I recognized the kids from the plane: they were trying to comfort Tai.

"Oh, no, we leave her alone for like an hour. *Quelle catastrophe* now? I don't see any toilet paper this time," De said. She was managing quite nicely to keep up her snide attitude.

"De, stop it. Maybe she's in real trouble," I said, making my way through the throng. Tai's eyeliner had dripped down her face in major thick globs. Her hair had come untangled and clumps were glued to her face. She was a certifiable mess. Between heaving sobs she managed to tell her story.

"There was this mime, and he was like imitating me? We were all like dancing around, so he'd have to dance, too? We were only having fun." She was sniffling ferociously and looked to the Bailey and Charisma bunch for verification. "So I bent down and turned around, and suddenly Kate told me that my backpack was open—I looked inside and my camera was gone!"

"Whew! Is that all, Tai? A camera's not so hard to replace." I started to feel calmer.

"And my wallet with my passport in it!" she finished. Oh no, this really was a catastrophe of major proportions. We all knew it.

"Did anyone see who did it?" De demanded of the group, who shook their collectively unkempt heads.

"Sorry," said the one I thought was Charisma—what's up with that name, anyway?—"like Tai said, we were all just caught up in the aura of the moment."

"The aura of the moment!" De was about to lose it. "Don't you know you have to be viciously aware of your surroundings in a foreign country? You never lose sight of where your passport is at all times. It's the most important thing you have on you."

I was about to remind De that just a little while ago in Alaïa, she'd been pretty caught up in her own aura. But I thought better of it. Time for the blame game later. We really had to deal with this now.

Luckily, a policeman came over and directed us to the prefecture to report the stolen passport. It seemed to take forever—Tai had endless forms to fill out. And with only De to help her interpret them, it was a hassle and a half. Finally, she was done and presented them to a dragon-breathing matron in wire-rimmed glasses behind the control desk.

"What happens now?" Tai, still hugely distraught and in desperate need of a tissue, wailed. "How soon can I get a new passport?"

"How soon?" The wire-rimmed warden showed a total lack of sensitivity to Tai's plight. "Ziss we cannot say. You come back tomorrow at *dix heures,* eh? At that time, we will check the *Objets Trouvés*—the Lost and Found—to see if it has been retrieved. So you return here tomorrow, eh?"

Okay, like I know this is being selfish and all—but tomorrow? That's when Josh would be back. My plan for tomorrow was to get up, get irresistibly gorgeous, and go to Josh's dorm. It did not include a sidebar to the police station.

\* \* \*

Aunt Lois and Uncle Robert were totally gallant, just like Daddy would have been. They were sympathetic and rampantly practical about the whole lost-passport thing. "You go back to the police station tomorrow," Uncle Robert advised, "and if the passport does not turn up, I will cut through the red tape—there are mountains of it here in Paris"—he chuckled knowingly—"and get you another. Don't worry. It is not the end of the world."

That was all De had to hear. She dashed back to her room to get ready for her date . . . I mean, sightseeing tour . . . with André. I almost felt like I should tell her to be back early. But I didn't. I also didn't remind her about calling Murray. If I didn't know better, I'd almost think she had totally forgotten about him.

What was that Out of sight, out of mind thing? Who'd said it, anyway? Yuck, I just remembered. Amber. I couldn't get rid of her, even when she was a zillion miles away.


After dinner—something Aunt Lois called cocoa-van but which looked and tasted just like chicken to me—I sat down to challenge cousin David at Nintendo. It felt just like home, being in my sweats, sprawled out in front of the TV, remote in hand. Okay, so it wasn't exactly *The Real World,* but I dug being with David. Even if he did beat me—like every single time. But what did I expect? Of course he was whip-smart and agile. Duh, he was family. It felt weird, even thinking that word: family.

"Cousine Cher! Are you letting me win?" he asked suspiciously, scrinching his exquisitely lashed eyes at me.

"Of course not, David," I told him. "I promise, you're winning fair and square. I'm just out of practice, that's all."

After the seventh round of Mortal Kombat, I was about to pack it in when Tai ambled into the living room. She was still in serious distress mode. "I feel like such a tard," she moaned, plopping down on the couch.

"Don't sweat it, Tai, it could happen to anyone."

"How come things that could happen to anyone keep happening to me?"

Truthfully? I often wondered that myself about Tai. But I had to cheer her up. "Come on, how about we do a lap and get some air?" I suggested as I got up off the floor. "It looks like a golden night. Maybe Dani will come with us."

Aunt Lois warned us not to go too far but suggested we might get a kick out of seeing La Fontaine Lamartine. "It's a park just across the street," she said, "and it is filled with people who go to the fountain, which is revered around the world, and fill their bottles with mineral water. It's quite interesting."

Tai was psyched to go, but Dani begged off to study. Our invitation reminded her of something, though. "Tomorrow is our last exam of the week, and a bunch of us are going to the Bois de Boulogne after school to celebrate. Why don't you come and hang with us?"

I didn't want to commit, pretty sure I'd be with Josh by then, but Tai was all, "Sure, we'd love to come, Dani."

"*Bien.* I'll meet you here around four, and we'll all go together," she said, and got back to her studying.

The park was just across the boulevard, as Aunt Lois said, and she was right about the fountain thing. There was this lineup of babushka ladies with empty mineral water bottles, filling them up. But how they could be sure about the water when the results of Josh's study weren't even in yet?

Tai interrupted my reverie. "Hey, Cher—look over there. Isn't that Dani's friend, the one who was so gallant to me at the party last night?"

I turned to see where she was pointing. Standing by a bench with an easel set up next to him was Jean-Michel. He seemed to be painting, but how much could he really see with just the gaslights above him? We walked over.

"Jean-Michel, hi!" Tai said, a little too loudly. She was stoked to see the one Parisian who'd been nice to her. Jean-Michel, startled, nearly dropped his paintbrush.

*"Mon dieu!"* he gasped. "Tai, Cher—I'm sorry, I was not expecting to see you here."

As Tai moved in closer to see what he was painting, I said, "We just went out for a walk. Isn't it hard to see what you're painting in the dark?"

Jean-Michel grinned and pushed his glasses up a little higher on his nose. "Yes, a little. I don't usually come out here at this time, but you know, the inspiration struck and what was I do to? I live just down the boulevard, so this was a close place to come."

I looked at what had inspired Jean-Michel. It was Dani. In the outfit she'd worn to last night's party. And it was a full-on likeness: he'd totally captured her bubbly spirit. Okay, so maybe I'm not a great art critic and all, but Jean-Michel's portrait of Dani looked almost as good as . . . well, in my opinion it was as good as any we'd seen at the Louvre.

I decided to take my shot. "That's hugely beautiful, Jean-Michel," I said gravely. "You really are in love with her, aren't you?"

"It's so obvious, eh?" he responded thoughtfully.

"It's obvious to everyone but her," I said. "Why don't you tell her?"

"Tell her? How can I tell her? We are not so direct as you Americans. Besides, Dani and I have known each other all our lives. She thinks of me as nothing more than an old, trusted friend. She doesn't see me in any other light."

Just then I got an idea. "What if you could get her to see you in another light?" I said carefully. "A more subtle, romantic light?"

"Cher, I am sure your intentions are the best," Jean-Michel said, "but aren't you forgetting that besides everything else, Dani already has a boy she loves? You met Claude, *non?*"

"That's just it. He's totally wrong for her!" I cried passionately. "Look, I don't know Claude very well, but even in the short time we've been here, I know this: He'll only hurt her." I could tell from Jean-Michel's expression that Claude probably already had. I bit my lip.

"So what is your proposal?" Jean-Michel asked.

"It's simple," I said, starting to feel the wave of absolute and total joy only the contemplation of a makeover could bring. "You have to present yourself differently. Think of it this way—you're an artist, and Dani has only seen one picture of you. It's time to paint another."

I didn't give Jean-Michel time to digest but rushed on. "You've got to start with your clothing." Jean-Michel looked down at his baggy pants. "Something isn't right with my clothing?"

I arched my eyebrows and tried to suppress a giggle. "Um, I'm sure it's really very stylish, but not very . . . well, girls like to see a little more of your . . . uh . . . form. Do you have, maybe, a pair of Guess? jeans that are a little more fitted?"

92

Jean-Michel looked doubtful but said, "I'm not much for fashion. I'll have to search the closet. Maybe."

"And your shirt," I continued, feeling more confident, "if you wore maybe a tight T-shirt . . ." I clarified, "It's like this, any time you can draw attention to your chest and shoulders, it's a good thing."

"A good thing? Girls like this? But you know, I'm not so . . . built up, eh? I might look silly."

I scrutinized Jean-Michel as best I could in the semi-darkness. It's true, he wasn't exactly Mel Gibson, but he wasn't Urkel, either. Underneath that baggy shirt, I was willing to bet he was harboring a muscle or two. Kind of like Josh; not muscle-bound but solid.

Tai interjected, "Cher's right, Jean-Michel, you should listen to her. She does wonders with makeovers. She turned me from a shlump into a Betty, practically overnight."

Jean-Michel wasn't sure whether to be impressed or distressed. "*Alors,* Cher, so let me get this right. If I do as you say, Dani will see a different picture of me?"

"*Absolument,*" I said, copying the way Dani said it, "But it's not just how you look, it's how you act, too. You'll have to make a few attitude adjustments."

"What kind of adjustments do I have to make?" Jean-Michel was starting to get all doubtful again.

"No biggies, don't worry. You don't have to go over-board, just do what any normal guy would do. Don't be too available. Don't call when you say you will."

"Don't call her if I promise to? Wouldn't that be rude?" I could tell Jean-Michel was never rude. How did he survive here?

"Not don't call her *ever*—just call her on boy time: about three days after you say you will," I amplified.

"And how will this help her to see me differently?" Jean-Michel still wasn't getting it. More input was needed.

"Well, she might suspect that maybe you have something else—or someone else—on your mind. If she starts to think another girl is after you, that's a good thing. Because once she realizes you are desired, she'll see you completely differently. Trust me!"

Jean-Michel looked anything but trusting.

"Listen to Cher," Tai insisted. "She really knows what she's doing."

Jean-Michel promised to think about taking my advice. Tai and I went back up feeling much better about the entire day.

# Chapter 10

*T*he next day I woke with a smile on my face. Josh was holding me tightly. I was nuzzled up against his chest, and we were dancing really slowly to that Cranberries song, *"Dreaming my dreams with you . . ."* Everything was perfect, until some clod jarringly put a cold hand on my shoulder and rudely interrupted. "Cher, come on. Cher, get up!" It was . . . De? Why was she cutting in on my dance with Josh?

De's breaking in on my ferociously exquisite dream set the mood for the morning. It wasn't a happy one. Not only had I totally overslept, but the primary event on my agenda was finding Tai's lost passport instead of finding Josh. I was so buggin' that at breakfast I actually scarfed down a butter-infested baguette. And that is *so* not me. Although it was crusty.

\* \* \*

While we were waiting at the police precinct, De dreamily waxed euphoric, recounting her evening with André. Tai was a rapt audience.

"It's so different when you do Paris with someone who actually lives here," De cooed. "He took me to the hottest restaurant in Paris. Of course, I let André order," she droned on, "and it was completely better than when we tried it ourselves." At that she snuck what should have been a guilty look at me but totally wasn't convincing. "I had coquilles St. Jacques—that's creamy scallops on the half-shell, and"—De giggled—"it tastes as smooth and romantic as it sounds, too."

Romantic? Hello? "Uh, De, maybe you want to rethink that description?" I said. "I thought you and André were just . . ." I didn't even want to say friends. "Acquaintances? And I was under the impression that he was just doing a props, taking you on a sightseeing tour. Which reminds me, you haven't mentioned any sights."

De narrowed her eyes. "Of course we're just acquaintances, Cher. What could you be thinking? If you hadn't slept so late maybe you'd know I even called Murray this morning." De was feeling totally righteous. It was my turn to ride the shame spiral. "I'm sorry, De, I didn't mean what it sounded like. André is kind of hot, though."

An assessment De agreed with just a little too enthusiastically. "Kind of! If I wasn't with Murray . . . Well, I know that he's just being gallant, but a girl could be sorely tempted."

De was still droning on when Tai realized like why we were here in the first place. She began apologizing profusely. "Cher, I'm really sorry. If I hadn't been partying with those kids, this wouldn't have happened. You could be with Josh now instead of standing here in this place with me."

"That's okay, Tai, it wasn't your fault. I still have plenty of time to see Josh. And when I do catch up with him, we'll make up for lost time. No prob." I aimed for light and breezy even though I wasn't feeling that way.

There was good news and bad news when Tai's name was finally called. Madame fire-breath informed us that Tai's passport had been recovered, but it wasn't here.

"Where is it?" Tai whined.

"Since it has identified you as *une américaine,* the passport has been sent to the American Embassy. You will have to go there to retrieve it," the clerk said.

I broke in. "Why would you send it there when you knew we'd be coming back here this morning? *You* told us to come back here!"

Old dragon-breath shrugged her considerable shoulder and said without rancor, *"C'est comme ça."* I didn't need De to translate. It was close enough to "Yeah, yeah, whatever."

Tai turned to me as we left the police station. "It's okay, Cher, you don't have to come with me. Go see Josh. We've already wasted enough time on this."

De was more than cool with that idea. "Tai's right. I'll go with her because this could take a while. When I told André"—why was she bringing him up again?—"about all this, he warned me that the French love paperwork and procedures. He said it's like what they live for."

De was all, aren't the French cute? It was like yesterday they were rude and obnoxious, but today she suddenly finds everything about them so adorable. Like André. When I didn't respond right away, she burbled, "Voilà! It's decided then: you go to Josh's dorm, and we'll meet later, back at your cousin's. Remember, we said we'd go to that picnic celebration with Dani and her friends. And, Cher—take this book of French phrases and translations. *Sans moi,* you might need it."

I couldn't really come up with a reason why I shouldn't go. By now Josh was sure to be back from that field trip.

"Cité Universitaire," I told the taxi driver in my best accent.

There was something different about the campus today. It was totally crawling with the backpack-and-flannel crowd. And even though this was a residential campus for all foreign students in Paris, it was all, here we are in L.L. Bean-land. Okay, so I know I looked a little out of place in my chunky-heeled Mary Janes and clingy Calvin Klein dress, but it was like the entire campus stopped to stare at me. I pretended not to notice and walked purposefully to the building called Fondation des Etats-Unis.

*"Mademoiselle! Vous êtes revenue!"* Pierre was still behind the control desk.

In the best possible combination of American and French—with lots of gesturing—I reminded him that he'd told me to return today. I asked which way to Josh's room.

"Josh, *mais oui,* of course. *La chambre est là-bas."* He pointed off to the left, but as I took a step in that direction, he stopped me, *"Mademoiselle—il n'y a pas personne ici maintenant."* Uh-oh. I had no clue what he was saying. Something about another person?

Pierre motioned to give him the phrase book. He instantly found the translation and pointed to it. He'd been trying to tell me that Josh wasn't here. After flipping through several more pages, he also got across that Josh was back from the field trip and had been there a few hours ago—but had gone out again with a group of people. It wasn't another field trip, Pierre was sure of that, but he didn't know where they'd gone. He couldn't predict when they'd come back, either.

I couldn't believe this. What was that joke Daddy used to make? "If it wasn't for bad luck, I'd have no luck at all?" If not for Tai's bad luck and her stupid lost passport, I would have been here this morning.

I suddenly had this totally empty feeling in the pit of my stomach. And it wasn't even for Josh. Right at that moment, I missed Daddy. I decided to give him a buzz, just to make sure he'd kept his chiropractor appointment. Only then I realized I couldn't. More than Daddy even, I missed my cellular.

By the time I got back to my cousin's, everyone was waiting to go to the Bois de Boulogne. Worse, everyone was all that Smashing Pumpkins song, *"Today is the greatest day I have ever known . . ."* Dani, who'd put her hair up in a bouncy ponytail and slipped into a pleated miniskirt, scoop-neck, and clogs, was all joyful about finishing her exams. "I have a good feeling that I did well," she said. "Pretty groovy, Dani," I agreed. "I bet you did."

Tai was ecstatic at having her passport back. And De was delighted at her own continued competency, explaining how she'd whizzed Tai through the whole scene at the American Embassy and how the whole procedure took like no time at all. After she'd finished accepting compliments due her, it occurred to all of them to ask about my little excursion.

Everyone acted all sympathetic. Except De was getting on my nerves with her I'm-so-good-at-this stuff. "Are you sure you understood what Pierre was saying?" She was actually challenging my communications skills.

"Of course I understood," I retorted, "even if I'm not up to your advanced level of second-year French."

"Chill, girlfriend, I was just trying to help."

"When I need your help, Madame Expert-in-All-Things-French, I'll ask for it."

"Whatever," De said, making the W sign.

Witnessing this little exchange, Dani giggled. At first I thought, My own cousin is mocking me? But then she made a gesture of her own. Using both forefingers, she formed the letter T and explained, "This is what we do when we say *'tout ce que.'* It means the same as you just did—whatever!"

Pointing out how much we really had in common somehow lifted my mood. It didn't bring me any closer to Josh, and I was just as pissed at De, but more and more, I liked being around Dani.

The Bois de Boulogne—Dani pronounced it Bwa de Boo-lone-ya—was major. Kind of like Griffith Park without the observatory. Or Central Park without the muggers. Dani said it was over two thousand acres, with a rose garden, a museum, two racetracks, a few lakes, and horseback-riding and biking trails. In honor of the end of exams, we were meeting her friends at the Shakespeare Garden—a place where all the plants mentioned in Cliff's Notes plays could be found. Not that I personally could recall any plants mentioned. But we didn't need any "to be or not to be" thorny branches to lead the way to Dani's friends. As if we could miss them.

They were like a roving pack of Parisian preppies. Practically everyone was in the same uniform as Dani: girls in pleated skirts, oxford shirts, and Hermès scarves; boys in khakis, polos, and brimmed berets worn backward. Except for one stand-out stud.

I was so totally psyched to see that Jean-Michel had already started taking my advice. Okay, so his shirt was still too big and iron-impaired, but he had dug up a pair of classic stovepipe jeans. And like, *vive la différence!*

But when Dani commented on them—she *had* noticed; my plan was working already—Jean-Michel affected this air of indifference. He totally did not even acknowledge Dani but put his arm around Tai and started to lead her around the garden, pointing out the plants and asking her if she knew what play they were from. As if! Dani seemed puzzled but not overly concerned.

"Let's get something to drink." She led me over to a picnic table where her friend Françoise and a bunch of others had set up a cooler and tray of sandwiches. I needed to get Dani talking about how different Jean-Michel looked, and I was just about to when her attention was rudely diverted. So was everyone else's.

Claude had arrived. Not in a subtle manner, either. He strutted over in skintight jeans, pointy lizard cowboy boots, tight T-shirt. Around his waist he was wearing Monique. Her Kenzo pants and jungle top were like painted on. Monique's toned arms circled Claude's neck, her shapely legs snugly crossed his waist. Her expertly made-up face was way too close to his. They were laughing riotously, as if Claude had just delivered himself of the funniest in-joke in the universe.

My first instinct was to be grateful that all Dani's friends were fixated on Claude and Monique and not on

Dani. The look on her face was one I'd seen before. Way tragic.

But to her extreme credit, Dani swallowed her humiliation and tried to pull it together. "He's tutoring her," she managed to say in lame defense. "I think they might be celebrating because maybe . . . Monique finally passed an exam?"

I was fuming. This is how a French boyfriend celebrates? By humiliating his girlfriend in front of all her friends? And Dani felt she had to defend him? The entire situation was way worse than I'd thought.

With some difficulty, the Velcro'ed pair ripped themselves apart, and Claude, freed of his human accessory, sauntered over to us. Dani wasted no time. "Claude, can I see you in private a minute?" she said quietly, attempting to grasp his elbow and lead him away.

He resisted. "But why?" Claude grinned and winked at me. "Whatever you have to say surely can be said in front of your American *cousine, non?* Rudeness does not become you."

Dani was vastly distraught. How could Claude have the gall—duh, I bet that's why they call them *Gall*ic—to make it even worse for Dani? Hadn't he totally embarrassed her enough? Dani didn't have a comeback for Claude, but Françoise did. In the truest tradition of t.b's the world over, Dani's came out swinging. *"Ça chingue,* Claude! It stinks that you would carry on with Monique—and right in front of us all!"

Claude never even ducked. "Carry on, what? *C'est absurde,* Françoise—what? I'm suddenly not allowed to laugh with a friend? This upsets you? It doesn't bother Dani—she can handle it, right?" With that, he put his overly developed arm around her and pulled her close to him. Dani squiggled away but didn't contradict him.

Mistaking her silence for agreement, Claude continued. "I came over to tell you that I can only stay a half-hour at most. Monique"—he glanced over in her direction—"is so grateful that my expert tutoring has helped her pass the exam, she is treating me to dinner. But we can hang out together for a while. The reservation isn't until later."

Did anyone but me see the tears welling up in Dani's eyes? I hoped not. This time, Dani didn't remain silent. She turned away. "No, we can't hang out at all, Claude. I have to go."

In a gallant attempt to salvage what was left of her pride, Dani turned and strode away purposefully. She never looked back but kept her eyes straight ahead. Unfortunately, she never looked down either, and she must have forgotten about the clogs she had on. She'd gotten no more than ten feet away from Claude when, suddenly, her legs were in the air, her butt was on the ground, and her clogs were flying off in every direction.

Dani had totally slipped on a pile of dog doo. The French rampantly let their dogs run loose, and the stuff is everywhere. Now it was all over Dani—not to mention what was left of her ego. I was horrified. I couldn't imagine anything worse. Claude, apparently, could imagine nothing more hysterical. He was laughing so hard, gripping his sides, he could barely come up for air.

Out of the corner of my eye, I saw Jean-Michel. It seemed that he had started for Dani, only to stop himself. Instead of helping her, he stood there and did nothing.

Françoise, Tai, and I rushed to help Dani up, while De and André grabbed toweling to clean her off. It was then I got that familiar sinking feeling. Had Jean-Michel done nothing because I told him not to be too available? Could he possibly have misinterpreted that to mean don't ever be gallant? No—I couldn't have screwed this up so badly, so quickly. Could I?

When we got home, Dani, who hadn't said a word the entire ride back, ran sobbing into Aunt Lois's arms. The two of them disappeared into the master bedroom. I thought Aunt Lois was a way cool mom, and her relationship with Dani was exactly the way . . . well, the way mine would have been with my mom. In all the time I'd been in France, I'd barely thought about my mom. I hadn't even taken the photo out of my backpack.

De came out to ask, did I think Dani would mind if she went out again with André tonight? Sometimes De was just beyond comprehension. I just looked at her and said, "Whatever, De. We'll be fine." De chose not to notice the sarcasm totally intended.

I went back to Dani's room and flipped on the computer. Finally—new mail from Josh.

"Ma petite Cher, I know it's been a while since I've written, but they've kept us so busy, I practically never have time to sit in one place and put my thoughts on the screen. Besides our field trips, we've been attending seminars, writing research papers, and keeping journals of our experiences. I have so much to tell you—I tried calling earlier, but your machine picked up. I figured you were out so I tried your beeper but still no answer—it's possible that the call didn't go through. Oh no, I'll have to continue this later, they're calling me."

He ended it, just like that. Without even his usual *Je*

*t'aime.* I couldn't help but wonder if the person who called him away so rudely had said "Joshie." I was just about to write back when Dani walked into the room. She'd scrubbed her face prodigiously, and with her makeup off she looked so young and innocent. I gave in to the urge to hug her.

"Is there a message from Josh?" Dani asked, glancing over my shoulder at the open laptop.

"He wrote—well, he started to, but he got called away. They're keeping him viciously busy." I wanted to steer the topic away from Josh and display sympathy for the mortifying events of the afternoon. But looking at Dani, I just couldn't. Her wounds were too deep and too recent. Besides, it seemed Aunt Lois had made giant inroads in that department. My mission became even more urgent. I had to point her toward the boy who really loved her and give Claude the pointy-toed boot. Tomorrow, I would.

"It must be so hard on you," Dani was saying, "to know Josh is so close but not to see him."

Hard on me? After what Dani had just been through? Not even.

"I have an idea," Dani said. "Since our examinations are over, I have only a little studying to do. What if, when I get home from school, I take you over to the Cité Universitaire and help you look for Josh? Maybe, at the very least, I can get more information for you."

Dani was being gallantly selfless. Instead of docking at humiliation harbor, she was already steering a new course, toward helping me. I was proud of her. And for some reason, the idea of Dani meeting Josh totally appealed to me. "That's so righteous of you, Dani—thanks."

*"D'accord,* then. *A demain."*

# Chapter 11

*B*y the time I got up the next day, Tai was already deep into the breakfast buffet. I caught her mid-croissant. "Good morning, Tai. I see we're going to need to do some prodigious work with *Claudia Schiffer's Perfectly Fit Buns* tape when we get back," I said brightly, pouring myself a mug of *café au lait*.

"I know, Cher," Tai managed to say between chews, "but they're so um-believable. They just melt in your mouth."

"Where's De?" I asked.

"Still sleeping, I think," Tai said as the last of the croissant disappeared into her mouth. "She got in mega late last night."

"Tscha! Like *you've* never come in after midnight, Cinderella?" De and her tart tongue swept into the breakfast room at the same time. Tai was all "I didn't mean anything by it, De. Don't detonate a hand grenade."

Virtuously filling up my plate with cantaloupe chunks, berries, and orange slices, I nonchalantly asked, "So how was it? Where'd you go last night?"

De dumped her 'tude and segued into faraway-dreamy mode. "We had the most golden night," she said, all breathless. "We went to dinner at this *très* Parisian bistro. It was a completely tourist-free *arrondissement*. I let André order . . ."

No, don't take me there. She'd better not describe the food in anything but the strictest of culinary terms.

". . . and then we went to le hottest disco in town," De continued, fluttering her arms, "where André taught me the mambo. The mambo is a totally classic dance. It's complicated to learn, but when you have an expert like André leading the way, you just fall into it." De was totally pleased with herself and reached for a baguette. "Tonight," she added, "we're going to a *très* sophisticated club."

That was it. I totally had to say something. "De, don't you think you're spending, like, a lot of time with André?"

I mentally ducked, expecting a typical De slice-and-dice attack. But it didn't come. Instead, De put her half-eaten baguette down and turned to me and Tai. Uh-oh, worse than imagined.

"You're right, I have been spending *beaucoup de* time with him." De was tossing in French phrases more capriciously than ever. "He's really kind of special," she said softly, and with a dangerously glazed look went on. "He's nice. Strong and muscular but soft and poetic at the same time." She giggled but then got serious again. "And he agrees with what I say—he doesn't always feel like he has to say the opposite, just to prove like he's the man and all." As if we didn't get the reference, she added, "And he doesn't call me woman. All that—it's nice for a change."

"Nice? Hello? Could you please connect me with the De I used to know? What always turned you on in a guy was that balance of brains and brawn, competition and eventual coming together. De, you know you totally thrive on confrontation. Especially when followed by an intense making-up period. Nice was never even part of the equation."

I was speaking the truth, and De totally knew it. The fabric of her and Murray's relationship is exactly what makes it special. It's like the two of them—bold, clashing, vibrant. Okay, so it's rough in spots but totally well-designed and engineered to last. Despite their differences, De and Murray fit together like classic outfits that never go out of style.

I'll admit that spending time with André had improved her command of French, but what about De's command over her own heart?

"It's not like I'm Jeepin' with André," she insisted. "We're like really good pen pals, only less geographically challenged."

I took one more stab. "De, he has a *tattoo*. Like four days ago you were freaked that Murray might get one, and now it's like attractive to you?"

"What can I say? A tattoo wouldn't be right for Murray, but with André, well, it came with the package." De dismissed me and this conversation. "So, zup for today?" Not waiting for an answer, she said, "'Cause I've got a bodacious idea. André says . . ."

With all the poetry-spewing, gourmet ordering, and

mambo'ing, I wondered how André had had time to say anything at all to her.

". . . we *absolument* cannot miss Versailles."

Tai must have been morphed with the guidebook last night, because she actually knew what De was talking about. "That's right, Versailles is way historic. We should see it." Turning to me—like as if I didn't know—she explained, "It's an um-believable palace where these all-powerful kings and queens lived. My mom's boyfriend said we have to go there."

"Well, then," I said brightly, "you should go. But I'm taking a pass."

De and Tai had the same thought and lit up. "You found Josh!"

"Not exactly . . . not yet. But when Dani gets home from school, she's going with me to Josh's dorm. No offense, De, but Dani thinks she'll be able to jump the communication gap and all. Maybe going with her will change my luck and he'll actually be there this time."

With the powerful sincerity only a t.b. could convey, De said, "I know he'll be there, Cher."

While waiting for Dani, I decided to give Daddy a call. I wasn't sure what time it was in L.A., though, and as I was standing by the phone calculating, it rang. Instinctively, I picked it up.

"Cher? It's Jean-Michel. I was hoping to find you'd be there."

"Where are you? Is everything okay?"

"All is fine. But I had to tell you. I can't go through with what you asked me to do. All night I could not sleep."

Dressing in cool clothes was keeping Jean-Michel up at night? I didn't get it. I didn't have to, as he elaborated.

"Not helping Dani yesterday. That was shameful. If in order to have her as my girlfriend, I can't be her friend, then it is not worth it. I love Dani too much to see her hurt. Yesterday, when she fell and I just stood there . . . *alors*, it is something I cannot ever let happen again. Do you understand, Cher?"

Did I ever. I explained to Jean-Michel that ignoring her when she really needed him wasn't what I meant. But it was just as well that he'd called.

"It's okay, Jean-Michel. Don't ever stop being her friend. But don't give up hope, either. Dani may just fall in love with you, yet." I didn't know how, but I was still determined to make that happen.

Dani was hyper-precise about when she'd be home, and we were Audi right after she changed. She seemed to have recovered from yesterday's brush with death by public spectacle and was all bubble and business on the metro. Negotiating with nasty ticket takers, doors that don't open by themselves, and changing trains came as naturally to her as shopping at the Beverly Center did to me. De was right about one thing: getting around Paris with a native did have its advantages.

Dani kept up a steady stream of bilingual chatter all the way. I marveled at her. Dani was definitely bright, completely popular, and had the best heart. But she let Claude stomp all over her and didn't even notice Jean-Michel. To her, he'd always just been there. Like Josh had always been there. Would he be there now?

Dani and I found Pierre manning his station. Did he like ever leave? When he saw me, he jumped up, bumping his bony knee against the desk. He started babbling excitedly. Dani matched him for speed, fevered tones, and gesturing. They finished off their conversation with a viciously limp-wristed imitation of a high-five. What was that about? Did it mean Josh was here? Or just that Dani had made a new friend?

Dani didn't make me wait for an answer. "Voilà, here's the story," she said. "Pierre knows you want to see Josh, but . . ."

Here it comes. Josh is, what? Off on another field trip? Testing water samples in the Aegean?

Noting the look of distress crossing my face, Dani sympathetically rushed on. "Josh left a short while ago. Pierre asked him where he was going, and Josh said, to dinner and then to a Greenpeace seminar. Pierre didn't get a chance to ask where the seminar was. But . . ." Dani's face held out a ray of hope. "I made a pact with Pierre."

Great. Dani made a pact with a geek. How that got me to Josh was a mystery, but only for a second, as Dani finished. "Pierre says he knows Josh will be here tomorrow morning. He will leave a message that an important package is being delivered, and Josh must stay on campus to receive it and sign for it. Josh will think it's from you! Then, all you do is come back here first thing in the morning, and violà, *you* will be the package— reunited at last with your love."

Dani was such a romantic! If she had any twinges of envy, she certainly wasn't showing them. She was totally into helping me hook up with Josh. I was bummed about missing him again but not so much that I lacked appreciation for the effort Dani and Pierre were putting in on my behalf. I was deeply disappointed but managed a smile.

As if Dani could read my mind, she said, "You know what, Cher? I have another idea. Let's go to a popular café where many Sorbonne students hang out. Maybe by chance we'll find Josh there. Besides, *j'ai faim*—I'm hungry!"

Dani's enthusiasm was almost catching. I thanked Pierre and followed Dani back to the metro. "We have to go up to the Latin Quarter," she said. "That's where the café is." I wondered if they served tacos and other Latino food.

"We're here," Dani announced as we turned the corner onto a street so narrow, my Jeep would never make it. I looked up at the sign above the restaurant. It said, Café des Deux Magots.

Okay, so I know there's a language barrier and all, but hello? It didn't sound like a particularly appetizing place to eat. I mean, maggots? And why would Dani think Josh might be here? He's PC, but he's not an eco-maniac.

Dani saw my doubtful look and assured me that this café was way historic, a prime meeting place for brainiacs. "Students come here and stay for hours," she explicated, "arguing politics and philosophy." Well, that *was* up Josh's intellectual alley. We sat down and I scanned the room. I didn't see Josh.

Dani helped me interpret the menu, and when the waiter came to take our order, I was pretty sure I was getting vegetable pâté and a salad, dressing on the side. Dani went for something that sounded high-tech but ended up being a steak. The waiter had adorable Josh-like dimples, and when he walked away, Dani looked at me and said, *"Et le survey dit?"* I totally understood. De wasn't the only one getting the hang of French.

It's uncanny how alike Dani and I are. Well, if you exclude our looks and sense of style—and the boy thing, of course. I was about to gently introduce the topic of Claude when I totally surprised myself by saying something else entirely.

"You seem to be really tight with your mother."

Dani didn't find this topic surprising at all. *"Oui.* She is *très sympathique.* I can tell her everything," Dani admitted. "And your papa, you can talk to him like a confidant?"

I thought for a moment. "It's not exactly the same, but Mel and I are pretty tight. We don't do that much actual talking." I could not have imagined running sobbing to Daddy if I'd been so brutally humiliated as Dani had been yesterday.

"Of course, it must be different," Dani agree. "You are, *après tout,* the woman of the house. You have to be more mature."

I was about to tell Dani how I take care of Daddy and all, but suddenly there was just something I had to know. "Dani?"

She looked up from her dinner. "When you and your mother talk, do you ever talk about *my* mother? Does Aunt Lois remember her?"

Dani wiped her mouth and carefully placed her napkin back in her lap. She picked up her glass of Perrier. It was this moment where like she knew what I wanted to know. And if she could tell me, she would. She tried. "Maman of course remembers your mother—they were sisters, after all. But that is something we hardly talk about. I tried, especially when we heard you were coming, but this look of sadness came over Maman. So I let it go. Maybe that is wrong of me." Dani tried to figure out if she'd upset me.

"No prob, Dani. You weren't wrong. I was just curious, that's all." I kept it light and breezy so Dani would understand that it was cool. Partly to get out of our embarrassingly mushy moment, I scanned the restaurant again.

That's when I saw him. From the back, that is. I'd recognize those curls anywhere—and that flannel shirt was totally from Josh's Seattle grunge collection. He was about a half-dozen tables away in a corner, sitting with two other student types. How long had he been here? My stomach suddenly had this total Marylou Retton backflip moment.

"Dani! That's him! Josh *is* here!"

Dani focused on where I was looking. *"Alors,* go to him—what are you waiting for?"

Carefully, I got up, smoothed out my skirt, and sucked in my stomach. Not that I'd gained any weight, but it had been a long time since Josh had seen me. As I approached the table, I caught the glance of the blond boy Josh was sitting with. Quickly, I put my forefinger up to my lips in a "Sshh" motion, to signal him not to say anything. I totally wanted to surprise Josh. And it's not like I planned this, but as I got right behind him, I impulsively covered his eyes with my hands and said in my most seductive, "Guess who?"

"I have *absolument pas d'idée,"* came the answer in a very thick French accent. *"Mais,* I cannot wait to find out!" What was going on here? Josh didn't sound like Josh at all. That's when he turned around, and I found out why. It wasn't Josh.

I was furiously embarrassed. I put my hands over my mouth and started to back away. "I-I-I'm very sorry," I stammered. And I never stammer. "I just thought you were . . . someone else."

Josh-who-wasn't-Josh looked at me way kindly, which made it even worse. *"Non,* it is I who am very sorry. You are quite beautiful. I wish I had been your Monsieur Guess Who." I was still backing away, hoping to somehow fall magically through the floor, when he added, "I hope you find him, for he is quite a lucky fellow."

Dani was all knowing sympathy and reached up to put her arm around me. *"Alors,* this has not been a great time for *les cousines.* We have both suffered our foolish moments."

Once again Dani had managed to lighten the moment. *"Allons-y,"* she said. "Let's be . . . Audi!"

I laughed and gave her a hug, "Let's be, then."

By the time we got back, De and Tai had returned from Versailles. Which had been a complete success. De coveted the red boots on some Louis XIV monarch, while Tai thought the Hall of Mirrors was totally on a par with the Fun House at Magic Mountain. "The stuff in the gift shop was awesome, too," Tai added.

Just then Uncle Robert walked in and, seeing the Versailles souvenirs, beamed his approval. *"Eh, bien,* it looks like you have managed to squeeze in some of Paris's history into your shopping trip?" he said in a good-natured way.

"Papa," Dani said, perking up, "were there any calls for me while I was out?"

"Let me see. . . . yes. Françoise, I think, twice."

"No one else—not Claude?" she asked, hopefully.

*"Non,* my sweetheart, not yet today." If Uncle Robert

realized this was, buzz, the wrong answer, he didn't let on. "I will leave you young ladies to your chatter."

But Dani's bringing up Claude in front of all of us was my opening. I slid in as gracefully as I could. "You've been going with Claude a long time, huh?" De and Tai knew what was coming next and snapped to.

"*Oui*. Our one-year anniversary is near." Dani was still in major denial.

I went on. "I know you explained about how Claude is from the right background and all, but have you ever considered that just being from the right background doesn't necessarily make him the right boy for you? Maybe you should think about someone more evolved?" I hoped I wasn't coming on too strong.

Dani bristled. "What are you saying? Of course Claude is right for me. Why wouldn't he be? *D'accord,* I admit he has been acting a little weird lately. This hasn't been the best week of our relationship. But he's not really like that. Underneath it all, he has a heart of gold."

Don't you mean stone? His reaction yesterday when Dani slipped belonged to someone with no heart at all. And she's defending him, yet.

I looked over to De for support, and she came through. "Dani, Claude is your first love, right?" she said softly. Dani nodded and De continued, "Have you ever thought that maybe your first love isn't destined to be your only love—or even your truest love?"

Tai picked up the ball. "Sometimes you meet someone, and you think, hey, he's cool, but for some reason, you reject him as a romantic possibility. So you go for someone else—except then it turns out that you've made a huge mistake." Dani was clearly clueless, which prompted Tai to go into a convoluted explanation of her own Travis-Elton-Josh-and-back-to-Travis spiral. Which totally took us off course.

Dani was all to Tai, "*You* liked Josh? But I thought—"

I was going to have to take this into my own capable hands. "Dani, remember when I told you about Josh? About how he was right there all the time, and I couldn't see it? And he turned out to be my true love?"

I rampantly hoped Dani would get the parallel but no such luck. De checked her diamond-encrusted Cartier—it was obviously time to get ready for her date with André, and she was running out of patience with Dani. So she just blurted out, "Dani, no boy treats his girlfriend the way Claude treats you. I know his type, though. He thinks he's all that. You need to dump this loser, like yesterday."

Uh-oh. De had gone overboard. Even I could feel the stinging sensation and the tears coming to Dani's eyes, but before I could soften the blow, Dani lashed out sarcastically. "*Merci bien,* Dionne. Everything was going along fine, and suddenly you arrive, and in the space of a few days you pronounce my boyfriend no good? And to think I looked forward to your coming." That's when the tears started to flow—prodigiously. De hadn't meant to come on that strong, but she had clearly hit a raw nerve.

I sat down on the bed next to Dani and put my arm around her shoulder. Through tear-stained eyes, she looked up at me. "And this is, of course, how you all feel. You think Claude is a beast." Dani felt betrayed, but she had to hear the truth from someone, and it didn't look like her friends were about to break it to her.

"Dani, listen to me," I urged gently. "Maybe it's *because* we're on the outside looking in that it's so clear to us. Claude may not be a beast, but he isn't right for you. There *is* a boy who is totally right, though."

Dani stopped sniffling long enough to eye me suspiciously. I plunged forward. "There's a boy who has always been there, just like Josh was for me, but you haven't been able to see him."

Dani still did not get it. A direct hit was the only option left. "Dani, it's Jean-Michel. He's been hopelessly sprung on you forever."

"Jean-Michel?" Dani's voice cracked and went up several octaves. She was incredulous. "But we are friends."

"So in Paris there's a law against friends falling in love?" Tai asked this in a way I could only hope was rhetorical.

"No, of course not," Dani said. I handed her a tissue. She had obviously never given Jean-Michel a thought before.

"Think about it, Dani," I said. "Jean-Michel is sweet, he's smart, talented, and he has a totally golden heart. People who love each other want the other person's happiness more than their own. And Jean-Michel would do anything to make you happy. You know he would. And once he learns how to dress, he can even be a Belmondo."

Tai then took it upon herself to reveal Jean-Michel's little secret. "Did you know Jean-Michel's painting a portrait of you?"

Dani was hugely surprised. She blew her nose loudly. "He is? He never told me that."

De tried to redeem herself by kneeling down in front of the bed by Dani. "Look, I'm sorry, I didn't mean to hit you over the head the way I did. It's true we've only known you a few days, but we already think of you as a t.b. And t.b.'s don't let other t.b.'s get slammed by the wrong guy, that's all. They also try to open their eyes to the right guy, if there is one. And in your case, the right one is in the park across the street right now, painting your picture, girlfriend."

Tai dittoed, "When we came back from Versailles, I took De into the park to show her the fountain, and Jean-Michel was right where we saw him the other night."

"Why don't you go out there, Dani," I urged. "Just go for a walk and see. You've said yourself that Jean-Michel is the kind of boy you could talk to about anything. Maybe it's time to talk about something really important now."

Dani seemed unsure but not unwilling. "Let me get cleaned up first," she said. "Maybe then I will go out." I gave her a hug.

# Chapter 12

*I* felt way better about starting to straighten Dani out, but it didn't help me sleep. Knowing I was finally going to see Josh kept me tossing and turning all night. I had to mentally reorganize my closet like six times before I drifted off. Even so, I got up viciously early. But that was okay. I needed the extra time to get ready. And three hours later, I was. The MAC makeup I'd decided on was perfect. The combination of Orb and Wedge colored eyeshadow looked totally natural. I did like an extra hundred strokes with the hairbrush and practiced flipping my shiny hair back and forth.

I was way grateful I had one romantic dress left for meeting Josh. It wasn't designer, but it was the total look I was going for: sexy and innocent at the same time. I'd seen it in this perfume ad billboard where the girl is like all flowing hair, running across a wheat-filled meadow into her boyfriend's arms. Which is exactly the way I pictured it would be with me and Josh. The dress itself was all crocheted. It had that faux-vintage handmade look, was babydoll short and sleeveless, all black, except for two blushy pink roses on the straps.

I don't usually do jewelry, except for some important pieces, but this dress screamed for a heart-shaped cameo on a choker. Luckily I'd run out to buy one just before we left for Paris. I didn't have any pictures small enough to fit inside the heart, so I just left the ones it came with. Josh would so not be expecting to see me in an outfit like this—duh, he wasn't expecting to see me at all. I tried to imagine his reaction, but all I could think about was the magic Parisian moment when he held me close in his strong arms and showered me with tender kisses.

"Girlfriend, that boy is not gonna let you go home once he sees you!" De's reaction when she saw me in the dress totally confirmed my choice.

"Um-believable," echoed Tai.

"Zup with you guys today?" I asked.

De was doing the André thing. "André's taking off from school. There's still so much he wants to show me." I'll bet, I thought.

Tai promised on Travis's most treasured skateboard that she would be totally careful, but she was, in fact, spending one more day with the alterna-kids. "We're going to this artsy area called Montmartre. I figured I could pick up a picture of Marvin the Martian for Travis or something."

Spare me the gory details. "Okay, I'll see you guys later. I'm not sure when . . . or if"—I smiled sneakily—"I'll be back. I mean, it might be late, so don't wait up."

De shook her perfectly manicured finger at me and

said in a mock-stern tone, "Don't do anything I wouldn't do." Which, of course, got me wondering.

I couldn't believe how jumpy I was on the way there. Every time we stopped for a light, I felt my stomach lurching. It was total chaos inside, and I was way grateful I'd skipped breakfast. I opened and closed my Vittadini bag like a hundred times, pulled out my compact, and checked for smudges.

The taxi crossed over the Seine River, and I could see those Bateau-Mousse boats going by. Maybe Josh and I would do that later. A romantic dinner cruise, just me and my hottie in the City of Lights. But Josh might have other ideas. After all, he's been here a majorly long time. I was suddenly hit with a vicious attack of the What If's. What if something's gone wrong with Pierre's plan and Josh isn't even there? This was my last full day and night in Paris. What if Josh *is* there but he's changed? What if he doesn't want to see me? I could feel a rash coming on. What if . . . Stop the tape, what am I doing? Of course Josh wants to see me—duh, didn't he say so in his last letter? I was mentally recomposing yesterday's letter when I realized we weren't moving. The cabbie was staring at me. *"Nous sommes arrivés à la Cité Universitaire.* This is where you wanted to go, *non?"*

I couldn't wait to see Josh, but something made me walk slowly toward his dorm. It felt like everything was suddenly all slow-mo. It was a picture-perfect day, almost like being in Beverly Hills but without the smog.

I figured Josh was probably in his room, waiting for the phantom package to arrive. So I was totally not expecting him to fall right into my field of vision. Except, suddenly there he was. And this time there was no mistake. Even though I was pretty far from him, I got a full-on frontal view. My heart was pounding. Because he was buried in a hardcover, he didn't see me, so I stopped for a minute to take it all in. I wanted to remember everything about this day forever.

Studying him, my nerves got all calm, and this complete love-rush enveloped me. That's how I knew the moment was here. My perfect Parisian moment. Josh must have sensed it, too, because just as I started my flowing-hair, slow-mo jog in his direction, he looked up from his book.

Only something was strange. He wasn't looking straight at me. Instead, he snapped his head all the way to the left, spun around, and dropped his book. I was about to wave and call his name, when I stopped dead in my tracks.

Someone *else* had come at Josh from the left, and in a flash, *she* was all in his arms. Her head was buried in his neck, so I didn't get a look at her face. Could be a hottie, could be a Monet—I couldn't tell. Was she, gulp, the Joshie girl? Josh was pressing her against him, holding her tight with one arm. He seemed to be stroking her flannel-shirted back with the other. The global Oris watch I gave him for our one-month anniversary glinted in the sun.

It must have blinded me, because I was like frozen. I was numb. When feeling did return, it was via a sharp stinging sensation in my eyes, followed closely by chunks rising in my throat. I kept blinking, trying to make sense of what I was seeing, but everything kept going all in and out of focus. Maybe it was a dream? Or a nightmare.

I don't know how long I'd been standing there, when I abruptly hung a U-ie, and started walking.

I had no clue where I was going or where I wanted to go. I just knew I had to get away from there. I wanted to erase the tape and start over. I couldn't possibly have witnessed what I just thought I did. It had to be a mistake. That probably wasn't even Josh. Only when I replayed the scene in my head, I knew it was him. The watch gave it away. I wished I'd never given it to him. I wished I hadn't come to Paris. I wished I'd never met Josh. I was all in flux.

As I walked, I passed cafés, kiosks stuffed with stupid Eiffel Tower souvenirs, and flower stalls. Random Parisians were rushing by, chattering animatedly, walking their dogs. How could everyone be acting so normal? Didn't they know the world had just caved in?

I needed to shop. And I needed it now. What was that faux-mall Dani had mentioned? Not the Galleria. Then it came to me. "Galleries Lafayette," I told the taxi driver. In no time, I was delivered to this humongously atrocious building. It was far from the Beverly Center, but there were eight levels a girl could get lost in. Which I totally intended to do.

As I weaved and wandered among the racks, I noticed that everything was color-coordinated. Red dresses with red scarves and crimson boots. Which reminded me of Amber. Before I could douse myself with Amber-repellent, her witchy words came flying back at me. "You think Josh is sitting around waiting for a little high school girl like you? Tscha! He's got all Paris at his feet." You forgot to mention the Parisienne all in his arms, I thought bitterly.

Could Ambu-loser have been right? How could everything have gone so monumentally wrong? I'd prepared so well for this trip, but nothing had turned out the way I'd planned. As I picked out an Hermès tie for Daddy, I tried to figure out what I'd done to drive Josh away. Maybe my letters to him had been too obvious. Maybe if I'd really read the books on his list, I could have discussed them intelligently when he'd called. Instead, I'd just gushed about high school stuff, how much I missed him, and gossiped about my friends. All I ever talked about was my world. Maybe all Josh needed was a trip into the global village to make him realize how different our worlds really were. Being in Paris had made Josh evolve so much, he didn't need me anymore.

Just when I didn't think I could feel worse, I thought of something else. Maybe Josh never really loved me in the first place. Maybe I was just convenient. Maybe to Josh I really *was* just some superficial Betty without a credit card limit or a clue. I was about to be swallowed into the looking glass of self-pity when I thought of Dani.

Well, at least there were some things I was still good at. Okay, I almost messed it up, but it was working out for the best. Getting Claude out of Dani's life and Jean-Michel into it in less than a week was a major coup. But how could I be so right about someone else's love life and so colossally wrong about my own? I took the blinders off Dani, but no one had taken them off me.

Power shopping wasn't making me feel any better. To top it off, I walked outside, and it was not only dark but raining. I thought about my makeup and my hair and of course my totally nonwaterproof Josh dress. Wet crochet is as soggy and uncomfortable as it sounds. Well, what did it matter now, anyway?

· The apartment was quiet when I got back. At first I thought no one was home. I started off in the direction of Dani's room, when I heard Aunt Lois call my name.

She came rushing out of the kitchen. "Cher! There you are. I was starting to worry. I know Dionne is out with André, and Tai phoned to say all is fine, but she is staying out a little later. So it was you I could not account for. But I see you stayed late to shop some more."

The expression on Aunt Lois's face changed radically from relief to concern as she lifted my chin to look into my eyes. It was a way weird moment. Confessing to a parent type about feeling wretched isn't something I normally do. I mean, with Daddy's cholesterol and everything. But the way Aunt Lois was looking at me, I felt like one of those transparent plastic dolls where you get to see all the body parts. I felt like she could actually see my heart and my hurt.

"Cher, you are dripping wet. Why don't you get out of those wet clothes, and put on Dani's bathrobe? I will pour you some hot cocoa." I hoped she didn't mean that cocoa-van chicken stuff—solids were not something I felt I could digest right now.

I tied Dani's powder blue terry cloth around my waist and trundled back into the living room, where Aunt Lois was waiting with a steamy mug of hot cocoa. She sat down on the couch and motioned for me to do sit next to her.

"I don't mean to be nosy, Cher, but you look so sad. What's the matter?"

I sipped my cocoa but didn't answer right away. Aunt Lois and Uncle Robert had tried so hard to make us feel welcome. I didn't want her to think the trip hadn't gone well. I tried for a perky grin, but what came out was a cocoa-mustached chagrin.

"Nothing. I mean, nothing earth-shattering," I answered slowly. "It's just, I guess, the trip didn't go exactly like I planned." I quickly tacked on, "But you and Uncle Robert and Dani and David have been so righteously hospitable to us. We really appreciate it."

Aunt Lois pursed her lips. It was like she had something to say but couldn't decide if she should. She went for it. "You know, Cher, I could always tell when something was bothering your mother. She was my little sister, after all. So much of you reminds me of her."

I looked into Aunt Lois's eyes and took a deep breath. "Tell me about her."

Now it was Aunt Lois's turn to inhale deeply. She looked away from me, toward the window, and began. "We were very close. It was as if one could tell what the other was thinking at all times. Our parents were quite strict and proper, so we relied on each other to keep secrets—and bend the rules a bit from time to time. We laughed a lot."

I wanted to ask about important things, like my mother's sense of style, but Aunt Lois was on a roll, and I knew enough not to interrupt. "She was the great beauty of the family, but she never gave a thought to her looks. She was too busy thinking about everyone else. Even though she was the youngest, your mother was the one who took care of all of us. Only she could get Papa to wear a woolen hat on snowy days and lift Mama's spirits when she was blue."

As I was listening to Aunt Lois, it hit me. So that's what Daddy had meant the night he'd said, "I haven't seen such do-good-ing since your mother."

"Something else you should know, Cher," Aunt Lois continued, "your mother was much more than a beautiful woman with a good heart. She was also brilliant. A scholar. Papa had high hopes for her. He wanted her to become an attorney."

I wanted to ask why she hadn't become one but married one instead. Aunt Lois continued, "We made a pact, your mother and I. We said we would raise our children together, so they could be as close as we were. We even had you and Dani about the same time. But . . ." Her voice trailed off. Then she took my hands and looked deeply into my eyes. "Who can say what might have been? No one knows. But I do know this, Cher." Her voice became strong and assured. "She would have been so proud of you. And not simply because you are so beautiful and popular. She would be proud of the person you have become on the inside. Of your sensitivity and how much you try to help others. In the course of one week, you have helped make Dani so happy. She's out with Jean-Michel as we speak."

I didn't know what to say. On the Richter scale of emotional days, this one totally did shake the earth. I was seriously drained. But there was one more thing I had to know. "Aunt Lois? I found something that I think belonged to my mother, and I was wondering if you knew anything about it." I went into Dani's room and took the photo out of my backpack.

Aunt Lois was hugely shocked. "Where did you find this?" I told her about coming across it in Daddy's desk drawer.

"I can't imagine why your father would have saved this," she mused. Realizing that was hardly an answer to my question, she let out another huge sigh and delivered. "This is Scott."

And Scott would be . . . ?

"When your mother was sixteen, she met Scott. He was a little older, really good looking. This photo does not do him justice. His family didn't have much money, but they were good people. Scott adored your mother, and they soon fell in love. They had so much in common. They both believed passionately in human rights. They went on peace marches and demonstrated for civil rights."

"It sounds like they were perfect. Why didn't they stay together?" I asked, feeling a twinge of guilt about Daddy.

"Oh, Cher, times were different then. As I said, Scott was older. During his second year at college, he decided to join the Peace Corps. He would go and your mother would follow. They would both devote a few years to helping the people of third world countries. It was very idealistic. But alas, idealism isn't all it's cracked up to be."

"Did Scott meet someone else?" I asked, thinking of Josh.

"Eventually, yes, but only after a long time. You see, our father forbade your mother to even consider the Peace Corps. He insisted she stay and go to college at home in California. And there was no way to disobey Papa. When he found your mother's application for the Peace Corps, he ripped it up right in front of her. It was terrible. After a year or so, she and Scott lost touch. But in the end, everything worked out. She went to college and met your father and fell deeply in love with him. And then you came along. She couldn't have been happier."

Aunt Lois handed me back the picture of my mother

and Scott. Suddenly, De's words took on way deep meaning. She'd said, "Your first love may not be your only, or truest, love." It seemed to be radically true. For my mom, for Dani, maybe for De . . . and maybe for me, too.

"Now it is my turn to get something for you." Aunt Lois got up and disappeared down the hall. When she returned, she said, "Ever since you got here, I wanted to give you something that belonged to your mother, but nothing seemed exactly right. But when you came in tonight, wearing that locket around your neck, I remembered that your mother had one just like it." Aunt Lois then produced a small box. Inside was a tiny, exquisitely perfect cameo locket. "Open it," she urged. On one side of the heart was a micro snap of my mom; on the other, my dad.

"Thank you, Aunt Lois. I'll treasure it forever." I clasped it tightly. "And thank you for telling me, you know, about my mom and all. It was way decent of you." Aunt Lois gave me a major hug and kissed me softly on the cheek. "This one is for me," she said. And then she kissed me on my other cheek. "And this one is for your mother," she whispered.

# Chapter 13

*I* had a lot to digest. It would take months to process. For one thing, it was going to be hard to look at Mom's picture and think of her as Disco Mom anymore. And the fact that she'd had someone in her life before Daddy was a monster shocker. But I was glad I had something important to dwell on. Anything that kept me from thinking about Josh.

Naturally, I spilled all to De, Tai, and Dani. I couldn't confess to Aunt Lois, but these were my t.b.'s. They were rampantly sympathetic and righteously indignant on my behalf.

"I can't believe you didn't go over and rip that Monet away from him!" De was totally steamed. I couldn't explain my inability to move, either. Normally, I'd be furious at Josh, but I hadn't reacted that way.

Dani was all "You came all the way to Paris, and Josh never even knew you were here. That is tragic, *cousine*

Cher. And when I think of how good you all were to me, it makes me feel worse for you."

"Um-believable" was Tai's comment. It came with a hug.

I totally refused to turn my last hours in Paris into a pity party, so I slapped on a smile and changed the subject. "So, De, how'd your last day with André go?" There was no sarcasm this time.

De plopped down on Dani's bed. "I don't know. I mean, it was fine. But spending a whole day with him was different than going out for a few hours at night. He is nice and all—very nice, but . . ."

". . . kinda boring?" I finished for her, gently.

De looked up. "Yeah. I hate to admit it, but you might be right, Cher. Remember when you said that nice was cool and all, but a girl like me needs more, you know, intellectual stimulation? Well, you were full-on bull's-eye, girlfriend. I thought about it all last night, trying to sort my feelings out. And you know what I realized when I got them all organized?"

I knew exactly what De was going to say. Tai, of course, didn't. De colored between the lines for her. "It was great being with André. I got much more out of Paris than I ever imagined. And maybe we will stay in touch and be friends. But when it comes to a man—in a heavy-duty sense—I have everything I need right under my nose."

Under your thumb, I wanted to say but didn't. "Murray is what I need. Maybe I wasn't all that sure before, but I am now. I just hope he didn't go and get that tattoo."

I chuckled. "Don't worry, De. Even if he did, you'll find a way to have it removed, I'm sure."

I turned to Dani. "And you and Jean-Michel? Details, girl! We need details."

"I think we will take it slowly," Dani said. "We have a lot to talk about. *D'accord*, it does feel right to be with him. Jean-Michel always knew how to make me smile." She blushed. "I thought I knew everything about him, but I never knew what a good kisser he was." She added, "Later we are going out Rollerblading. I'm teaching him how." I thought about Jean-Michel falling on his butt trying to impress Dani and how Dani had slipped on hers in front of Claude. It seemed like Dani and Jean-Michel were both on their feet now.

*"Alors,* ready to go, girls?" Uncle Robert had come into Dani's room to hurry us along. "The luggage is in the limo, and the chauffeur is outside waiting." We'd decided to do this trip with only one limo, so Aunt Lois, Uncle Robert and cousin David weren't coming for the ride. Just Dani and Jean-Michel were accompanying us to the airport.

The good-bye scene at the apartment was mercifully brief but not without its fabric-crushing moments. Only cousin David didn't try to squish me into oblivion, though he did make me commit to a Mortal Kombat rematch to be played at a future date. "Any time," I told him, and gave him a smooch on the top of his head. I even gave the dog, Gigi, a friendly good-bye pat. Uncle Robert hugged us all prodigiously, as did Aunt Lois. We thanked them profusely. They had been primo hosts.

When Aunt Lois noticed that I was wearing the new cameo locket, she kissed me again. *"Bon courage,* Cher."

Saying good-bye at the airport was way more heart-tugging. Okay, so Dani was this cousin that up until a few months ago I didn't even know I had. But now that I did, well, I didn't want to lose her. The idea that I might not see her again sent shivers up my spine—like the way I'd felt when Tai went to New York and I thought she was gone for good.

"Dani, you are *so* totally coming to visit me in Beverly Hills," I commanded. "I will not take no for an answer."

*"C'est bien,* cousine Cher," she said as tears welled up in her cornflower blues, "because I wasn't planning to say *non.* Of course I will come—I can't wait." Jean-Michel looked on, beaming, as we formed a hug huddle. Dani wiped her eyes and, pointing us toward Customs, said, "Have a good trip. And, Cher . . . I don't know how I know this, but with Josh . . . ?" The mention of his name was enough to send me into a tailspin. *"Alors,* I know it will work out somehow."

I didn't believe her for a second, but I did believe she meant it.

There was this homecoming team waiting for us at LAX. As I'd predicted, Murray was all there, and he and De launched into a major PDA attack. She rushed into his arms, and he planted a big wet one on her, completely messing up her lip-liner. But De didn't seem to mind a bit. When they unlocked, Murray pointed to his left sleeve, which was rolled up just past his bicep.

"I have a surprise for you," he said, beaming impishly.

De was all, "Oh, no, you didn't! If you got a tattoo, Murray . . . Where's the cellular? I am calling your mother right this second!"

Murray laughed. "I knew that's how you'd react. Woman, is there anything I don't know about you?"

I was thinking, yeah, plenty.

But then he unrolled his sleeve, and what came

tumbling out was the most bodaciously glorious crystal drop necklace. Exactly the one De had been coveting. I had a feeling De's thank you was going to be long-lasting and profound.

Murray had done another props. He'd brought Travis to the airport to meet Tai. And Travis, eternally empty-headed, did not come empty-handed. Tai was just about to throw herself at him when he shoved something in her face, nearly suffocating her. It was a huge, furry Marvin the Martian doll. "This is for you," Travis said shyly. Tai hugged the doll and looked up at Travis, all doey-eyed and misty. He put his arm around her and they started off toward the exit together.

Even though my own love life was like bring on the wrecking ball, I felt totally good about the reunion scenes of my friends. De and Murray, Travis and Tai. First loves, true loves, whatever. They so belonged together.

It's not as if I was left stranded at the baggage claim all alone. Daddy had come to surprise me. He gave me a giant bear hug. "I missed you, Cher. The whole house-hold did, too. I'm glad you're back, all in one piece." No way could I tell Daddy that one piece wasn't exactly the condition my heart was in. So I planted a wet one on his cheek and said breezily, "I'm glad to be home, Daddy." I so meant it, too.

"I have a surprise for you," Daddy said, as we turned into the long driveway toward our house. He pointed at the six-car garage. "Oooh! Daddy, you got me a new car!" Only that wasn't it. Exactly.

"You're a woman of the world now, and you should have a driver's license. So I scheduled your driving test for next Saturday. I know you'll pass this time. I have ultimate faith in you, Cher."

"Solid, Daddy. I won't let you down." I knew I wouldn't, either. After all, it wasn't like Josh was going to distract me this time. Soon as we got inside, I gave Lucy a peck and ran upstairs to bond with my cellular. I had so totally missed it.

"Oh, Cher?" Daddy called as I got halfway up the steps. "Josh left a message on my phone. He said he'd been trying to reach you but wasn't getting an answer on your line, and your beeper didn't seem to be working. Didn't you see him when you were over there?"

"Um, kind of, but not exactly. It's a long story, Daddy. We were really busy getting culture."

"Not too busy to shop, I see," he said, as he surveyed the mountain of luggage José was helping to haul into the house.

Over the next few days, I thought about Josh. And I thought about what Aunt Lois had told me about my mom. It was way inspirational. I mean, if my mom could get over Scott—and they were together, like, years— getting over Josh would be a piece of fat-free cheesecake. Tscha! Was I my mother's daughter, or what?

I started with the physical stuff. I put Josh's picture in the bottom drawer of my old dresser. Facedown. I donated all the books he'd given me to the homeless shelter in South Central. I mean, everyone could use a little existentialism, right? Every time I turned on the computer and saw the message "You have new mail," I pressed Delete. It kept asking me, "Are you sure you want to delete this?" Hello? Computers could be so thick sometimes.

The hardest thing was having to let the answering

machine pick up the calls. I didn't want to take a chance that it might be Josh. Then I'd have to talk to him. I wasn't ready for that yet.

"Cher, it's De. Pick up, girlfriend."

I switched off the machine. "Zup, De?"

"I think you're taking this getting-over-Josh thing too far, too fast." De never wasted time with preliminaries if she had something important to say.

"What are you talking about, De? I thought you were with me on this."

"Of course I am, Cher. But as your oldest t.b., I owe it to you to tell you how I really feel." De laid it on the line. "I think you should return Josh's calls. He deserves to know what's up, Cher. I mean, have you considered the possibility that what you saw *wasn't* what it looked like? It's not like you haven't made mistakes before, Cher— remember when we were in New York and you thought he was all with the 'Mental, Mental' girl? I'm strongly advising you to call him."

I could barely believe what I was hearing. And from De yet. It was all I could do to stay calm and rational. "Okay, so that 'Mental' stuff *was* all in my head. But this time, duh, a bodacious Betty rushes into his arms and nuzzles his neck. He's stroking her back. I saw it. What part of that could I have misinterpreted?"

De didn't have an answer, but I sensed there was something more she wanted to say. After a moment of strained silence, she interrupted this program for an important bulletin. "Josh called me today."

"He *what??* De—you didn't say anything to him, did you?" I trusted De, but I went on full-scale alert.

"Of course not, Cher. What do you think I am? But he sounded so . . . I don't know, confused or something. He was worried about you. I felt bad for him."

"You felt bad for *him?* The sympathy cards are over in this aisle, girl. So what did you tell him?" I demanded.

"I didn't commit. I did all vague and stuff. Told him you were fine and all but not much else. Never said we were in Paris. But I promised to tell you that he called."

"You did good, De. Thanks."

I hung up and considered De's advice. I rejected it. No, I'm not calling Josh. The best thing to do is get over him and get on with it. Better that the whole thing happened now when I'm still the undisputed queen of Beverly Hills teendom. I have my whole life in front of me. And I am more determined than ever that it's going to be golden. From now on, it's going to be like, Josh who?

# Chapter 14

*E*very day after school for a whole week, I practiced for my driving test. Murray helped me. I felt a special thrill getting behind the wheel of my loqued-out Jeep again. I hadn't realized how much I'd missed it. The Jeep missed me, too. It wasn't born to sit in a six-car garage. It needed to be out on the open road, with a Betty like me in the driver's seat.

On Saturday Lucy had my most capable-looking outfit ready. She did not want a repeat of last time's fiasco. "All systems go," I said. I gave her a thumbs-up as I took a last sip of fresh-squeezed and headed out the door to the test.

Okay, so the first sign of "Houston, we have a problem" was when the tester slid into the seat next to me. It was the messiah—the same blubbery impatient king of all things Motor Vehicle who'd called me girlie and failed me last time. Like what are the odds of that? And it wasn't as if he didn't remember. He gave me a stare that was all *"You're* back?" and started writing something on his clipboard before I even turned on the ignition.

I was all I am *not* going to let tester Girlie-man throw me off. I'm simply going to demonstrate my driving skills, which are totally superior. "You ready?" he asked. I nodded.

I was doing great, driving straight and all, staying precisely between the lines when he said, "Make a right here."

"Here?" I repeated.

"What part of that didn't you understand?" he said facetiously, again indicating the next corner. I swallowed hard and made the turn. "Cut the wheel, you're in the oncoming lane!" he yelled. Okay, so my turn might've been a little wide. But this is the street Josh and I drove on the night he'd rescued me after the hold-up. It's where we turned to get take-out for Daddy and the lawyers working late. I remember how Josh had looked at me that night, all "That's a really thoughtful idea, Cher." I bet he's saying the same thing to Ms. Nuzzle-Neck right now—*en français,* of course.

"Slow down, you're coming to a light." It was like tester Girlie-man was just waiting for me to mess up.

"I totally saw it. I was slowing down," I said, giving him a competent but ravishing smile.

"All right, pull into the next street and stop in the middle for a three-point turn," he said. I was midway through point two when I looked up and saw the billboard. It was that perfume ad, where the girl in my dress was running through the wheat field toward the guy. How could I not have been distracted by that? I just tapped the fire hydrant lightly. It sounded worse than it was. There wasn't even any damage. Girlie-man didn't say anything this time. He just kept writing.

I was determined to pay scrupulous attention for the rest of the test, assuming there was a rest this time. "Head back to the DMV" were his only instructions, delivered in a monotone. He didn't mention which route to take, so I figured, Rodeo back to Wilshire. Maybe passing Giorgio would bring me some luck. I executed the most golden right onto Rodeo, but when I came to the four-way Stop sign—like who was the sadist that invented those, anyway?—I saw two cars totally going at the same time. The Porsche Carrera, driven by an anorexic bouffanted Hollywood-wife type, was directly in front of me. She was reprimanding the child in the seat next to her, who, I noticed, was not wearing a seat belt. She never saw the Rolls Corniche on the right start into the intersection. She gunned the engine.

In a battle of the luxury cars, I knew the Porsche was toast. It would totally end up with a nasty dent. Instinct took over, and I hit the horn really hard. "Hey! Watch out!" I stuck my head out the window and yelled. "Don't you know it's like yield to the dude on the right? And put that kid in a seat belt," I added for good measure. I thought about saying something about her hair, but I figured I'd messed up my test enough.

I was wrong. I mean I was righteously, furiously wrong. It turned out that Girlie-man was totally impressed by my alertness and ability to ward off another person's accident. "Looks like you gained some maturity since your last test," he said almost admiringly. "And lots of culture, too," I said, beaming. He passed me.

\* \* \*

I have to admit that driving to school legally wasn't the same kick as when I went with just my permit. But De, Tai, and Murray were "All right, Cher! Welcome to the club." There were limp-wristed high-fives all around. Of our group, only Travis remained license-challenged, but when you thought about it, that was probably—duh, definitely—for the best. Until they gave out licenses for three-point turns in outer space, Travis's skateboard remained the safest way for him to travel.

The only person at school who didn't bask in my reflected glory was, big surprise, Amber. Spring break had done nothing to smooth the edges off her rampant jealousy. "So I see you survived your brush with culture" was the first thing she said when I got back to school.

"Which is more than I can say for your brush with rhinoplasty," I retorted, noting how Amber had obviously spent her week. It was her third crack at nasal perfection, and the bandages were still fresh. "But hey, maybe third time's the charm." I winked and quickly added, "Or maybe three strikes and you're out."

"Cher, isn't it time for your oral?" It was Hall-Geist, attempting to get our attention. I was actually in overtime. I was supposed to have given it the week we got back, but I wasn't fully prepared. I was still towup over Josh. Hall-Geist had agreed to give me another week.

I'd worn one of my authentic new Parisian purchases just for the occasion. Visuals are so critical when you're doing an oral. I picked a short, champagne Armani, my new Gucci boots, and topped it off with a jaunty peach beret.

"Okay, so my topic is 'How the French Are Misunderstood.'" I checked to make sure everyone was paying rapt attention. Except for the Iranians in the back, they were.

"You know how everyone always says like, 'Don't go to France, because the Parisians are so totally rude and all'? Well, on my cultural fact-finding mission to Paris, I learned that their bad rep is grossly undeserved. It only seems like they're rude because of the culture gap. Like, they don't understand why in a store, we're all grabbing things off the racks and trying on like six things at once. It's their country, all right, and when you go there, you have to do things their way. Once you learn to sweetly point at what you want and let them bring it to you, they're totally nice. And once you speak the universal language—and I am referring to plastic, *naturellement*—they're extremely helpful." I looked up from my notes to make sure everyone was still with me.

"And in conclusion, may I remind you, that in a voracious act of mass generosity, they gave *us* the Statue of Liberty. And no matter how many pigeons have landed on it, and how much graffiti has been sprayed on it, they've never once tried to get it back. Thank you." Feeling way satisfied with my presentation, I sashayed back to my seat. Hall-Geist had to deliver an A for that.

There was complete and utter silence for at least thirty seconds. Wow, I'd really stunned them with my brilliance this time. Hall-Geist probably realized he was like going to lose everyone's attention if he didn't say something fast.

"Does anybody have an opposing view?" is what he came up with. "Most of this class has traveled overseas. I want to hear your opinions. Or does everyone agree with Cher?"

Amber's arm shot up. Before he could even acknowledge her, she was all, "Agree? As if! Mr. Hall-Geist, I can't believe you're going to let her get away with this lame oral."

Lame? Hello? What oral was she tuned in to? Mine was totally global. Which is what I told her.

"Well, excuse me, your Cher-ness," Amber drawled, "but I don't see how your oral was well researched, well organized, or well thought out."

"Is that the problem?" I shot back. "Well, you can be excused for not seeing, Ambu-luckless. Who wouldn't be blinded by the cacophonous clashing of your— Would you actually call that an ensemble?" The whole class roared in approval of my put-down. Even the Iranians stopped mid-Farsi to bow to my witty repartee.

Amber, desperately in need of an ally, turned to Hall-Geist. "I think she deserves a C. Or less."

A C? As if! "What's your real problem, Amber?" I asked as I passed her in the hallway after class. "Are you all like, 'Dear Diary, I don't think Elton likes me anymore'?"

I totally don't know why I said that, but uh-oh, my bad, I hit a nerve. Amber came back with a one-two punch that was way harsh. "Maybe Elton and I *have* hit a rough spot in our relationship," she said, bandaged nose up all in the air. "But at least I didn't run all the way to Paris just to catch my boyfriend with another girl."

I suddenly felt wretched. The high I was on from my stellar performance in class evaporated. So now what? The whole school knew? How could this be? My stock would totally plummet. On a scale of lame comebacks, mine to Amber was lower than zero. "Josh and I have both matured," I said. "We've grown apart, that's all. Besides, I have much more vital things to do with my time than pine over grunge-boy, anyway." I didn't wait to hear Amber's reply.

# Chapter 15

*A*ll my t.b.'s were totally gallant about helping me forget Josh. It's like I'm the one who usually helps everyone, but now everyone's united in this giant helping huddle on my behalf. They're trying to keep me mega busy.

Yesterday Christian invited me to the Beverly Center. "How 'bout you drive, cream puff?" he'd said. "More room for packages in your Jeep, you know what I mean?" It sounded like a good idea, but as we trolled the most upscale mall in all Cali, everything reminded me of Josh. I mean, Eddie Bauer furniture? How much more Josh could you get? And was it my imagination, or was the Gap really doing a flannel display window? Hello? This is Beverly Hills, guys. Get a clue.

Christian had steered me toward the free-standing espresso bar and planted me at a tiny table for two. "So, Cher, babe, shopping is obviously not happening for you today. *Très* symptomatic." Ever since we'd gotten back from France, Christian and De were playing the who-can-throw-in-more-French-phrases? game. It was totally boring.

"Plus, I been noticing you spending *beaucoup de* time at home, not making the scene every weekend. Is it that bad, honey?" Christian was all blue-eyed empathy as he cupped my chin.

"Tscha, Christian, don't be silly. I'm choosing to spend more time at home, that's all. The household still has not recovered from my absence." Hello, that was a lie, and Christian knew it.

"And now that I'm culturally aware, I need time alone to explore my inner self." Yuck! Who said that?

To his t.b. credit, Christian didn't laugh. He just nodded. "The nesting vibe. Cool, I can dig it. But look, Cher, I know what it's like to be dumped. It hurts. But just because you got your heart stomped on doesn't mean it can't mend. I've always found that the best antidote is finding another boyfriend."

For him, maybe. "Christian, I honestly appreciate your concern, but finding a boyfriend is so totally not on my agenda. I'm swearing off guys for a while and working on myself."

"What's to work on, Cher? You're perfect just the way you are." If only. Not perfect enough for Josh.

I dove into my schoolwork with unbridled passion. It was paying off, too. My teachers were stunned. Instead of negotiating for A's, I was actually earning them. That's how Daddy knew something was wrong. "What's with all the studying, Cher? You used to be so social." His brows were all knitted together. I reminded him that college was just around the corner and it was important to develop good study habits while I still had time. He couldn't disagree with that.

But school can only take up so much of your time. It's not like I really had to study that hard to get A's. I had an intense amount of excess energy to burn, and no clue what to do with it. Shopping wasn't helping, and I'd sworn off boys. So what was left? Plus, I didn't want to do just anything. I was looking for something uplifting—and something that would keep me busy on Saturday nights when all my friends were out on dates.

I turned to the portrait of my mom for inspiration. And that's when it hit me. Duh! Helping humankind. Community service. I could do that. I *had* done that. Okay, so before it was because Josh had made me feel selfish and I wanted to prove him wrong. But now I know that the desire to help humankind is in that DNA stuff, deep inside my own designer genes. Didn't Aunt Lois say that my mom was all for those third world countries? Who knew they even had third world countries in those days?

But what would my community service be? I mean, joining the Peace Corps was out. I totally did not have the wardrobe for it.

I asked Geist-Hall to run down my options. She ticked off a list: Bosnia, the homeless, the clean-up-and-take-back-our-streets effort. But it was all been there, done that. I wanted something different, something more suited to my personal skills. And then she hit it. "How about SafeRides, Cher? I heard you got your driver's license."

SafeRides, perfect. That was the permanent designated driver on call thing. Like kids could call you from a club or a party or something when they weren't in any condition to drive. You'd pick them up from wherever and take them home. Safely. It fulfilled my every need. I'd be using my newly minted driver's license for a good cause, not just for shopping sprees. And who knows how many teen fender-benders I'd help avoid? As long as they finished puking before they got in my Jeep. Plus, the SafeRide phones were busiest on Saturday nights. I felt a surge of energy. "Where's the sign-up sheet?" I asked.

"SafeRides. What is your location?" That was pretty much all the training I needed. I joined a bunch of other kids in the high school guidance office, which had been set up as headquarters. Okay, so like these weren't the kids I usually hang with on Saturday nights. Did they even go to my school? They weren't part of any clique I knew.

"SafeRides," I said competently, my first Saturday night on the job. "What is your location?"

It was Paul Devere, the famous pool puker. He was way polluted and needed a ride home from some random fiesta in the Valley. As if! "Uh, could someone else take this one?" I looked around hopefully at my fellow volunteers. Okay, so it was clear we were all here for the same reason. None of us could get a date. In my case it was a choice, but for these kids, the choice had been made for them. Long ago. But I was way grateful for the girl in the ripped 501s who perkily agreed to go fetch Paul. I resolved to help her with hair and makeup when she got back. Hmm, now there was another idea. I could redo all these kids while we were waiting for calls. Two ways to help humankind. And at the same time. I was getting way good at this community service stuff.

"SafeRides. What is your location?"

"Right around the corner, cutie pie," came the response. "Can you come pick me up, pretty please?"

It was Elton. And he was totally straight and sober. "Elton, what are you doing? Don't tie up the phones if you don't really need a ride."

"Oh, but I do. Only if it's from you, Cher babe. And besides, there's call waiting on those phones. All the toasties will get through just fine. So what do you say, come and get me?"

"As if, Elton. Go home to Amber." I was about to hang up, when he confirmed, "Last Tuesday, babe. Amber's last week's Snapple. Which is what I heard about you and that college creep, too. So I figured, hey, fate has brought us together to try again. Do you believe in fate, Cher?"

"What I believe, Elton, is that you are totally fated to spend another long night in your Corvette, alone with your CD player. I hope you've got lots of Alanis Morissette to keep you company. I don't know what you heard about me or who you heard it from, but you were never very good at that game of telephone." I hung up. A few minutes later, another phone rang.

"This one wants to talk to you, Cher." My SafeRides *compère* at the desk in front of me indicated to pick up line 4. Elton is so persistent!

"Tell him I left," I said.

"It's not a he, it's a she—and she says it's critical."

I knew right away. "De?" I was all full of concern. "What's the matter, did you and Murray have a fight? Do you need me to come for you?"

"Chill, girlfriend, I didn't mean to scare you," came her response.

"Where are you? What's going on?"

"Murray and I are in Malibu, and my cellular rang." I waited for the punch line.

"Cher, it was Josh. He got back to L.A. today."

"And he was expecting maybe a Welcome Home fiesta?" I managed weakly, but De knew that underneath my tude, I was way trembling.

"Cher, listen to me. He had me on the line, like, forever. Murray was getting all impatient. Josh kept saying how he didn't understand why you're dodging him. He was like, 'First, she's writing me love letters and sending me cookies, and suddenly, without any warning, I'm out of her life?' He was all 'What happened, De? I know you know. Did Cher meet someone else when I was away? Is that it?' "

I was thawing fast but determined to get a grip. "If you didn't tell him anything, De, I'm sure he'll get the message and stop calling you. I'm sorry he bothered you again."

Maybe it was De's being with Murray that kept her all romantic. But it was like she was taking Josh's side. "You've got to talk to him, Cher. Look, here's the way I see it. Maybe he was seeing someone else—briefly—in Paris. But it was obviously meaningless, and it's totally over. It's not as if you don't know what it's like to be tempted, Cher. Remember Griffin in New York?"

I didn't know how De could compare that meaningless flirtation—unless she was really thinking about herself and André in Paris.

De was all "Josh is here now and he wants you. He's begging, Cher—it's pathetic."

"What's pathetic," I shot back, "is me going all the way to Paris because I thought he missed me. Not even!"

*   *   *

The next day Josh showed up at the house. I guess I was kind of expecting it, because I kept a vigil by the bay window in my bedroom. When I saw him pull up, I buzzed Lucy. I reminded her that if she let him know I was home, her Ben & Jerry stash was Audi.

"But her car's in the driveway," I heard Josh saying. Lucy suddenly had trouble with the language. Josh had no choice. He left. The quick glimpse I got was enough to see that he looked totally hot. He'd even shaved his goatee. The influence of Ms. Nuzzle-Neck?

Okay, so I know it sounds like I'm acting way harsh and all. But if Josh could break my heart once, what's to stop him from doing it again? I was pretty confident I could get over him now—but I didn't feel so sure about a second time.

# Chapter 16

*C*ome on, Cher, ya gotta go with us." Tai was on my cellular, and she was pleading. By some weird twist of fate, Travis had scored a bunch of tickets for a concert next Saturday. And for some reason, Tai thought my going would be a good thing. Even she and Travis were starting to get concerned about my lack of a social life.

"It's really proper of you and Travis to think of me, Tai, but I'm committed to SafeRides for Saturday. They need me there."

"That SafeRides thing is totally vital," Tai acknowledged, "but I'm sure they could get along without you for one night. Besides, we need you, too, Cher. We really miss hangin' with you. Weekends aren't the same anymore." Tai was getting major sappy on me.

"May I remind you, Tai, you see me every day at school."

"School doesn't count. We never have any fun together anymore."

And Tai thought going to a concert with a bunch of toasties was my definition of fun? Not even! I reminded her that it wasn't my scene. "I totally appreciate what you're doing, Tai, but wouldn't you guys rather ask someone who's into this kind of music?" I'd actually zoned out when she said what group it was, figuring, some crybaby college combo, or at the very least, grunge wannabes.

"But, Cher, it's the Cranberries. You *do* like this kind of music."

"Tai, I know, like, *one* song—"

She didn't let me finish, "And you like that one song! The rest are just like that one, only better. When you hear them sing "Zombie," you'll totally lose it. It's so intense." And Tai thought this was like a convincing argument? My reluctance was coming over the wireless loud and clear. Yet Tai would not be turned away.

"Cher, remember when you and De came to New York to get me? I didn't call you or anything, but you sensed somehow that I needed you. And you got on a plane and came for me. Well"—she took a deep breath—"we're sensing that you need *us* now. You need a night out, you need to be with your t.b.'s and have fun. We need you to let us help you, Cher."

Where had this conversation gotten off the freeway and onto a road less traveled? Somehow, Tai managed to turn everything around so that if I didn't go to the concert, I like wasn't helping them or something? Maybe by osmosis she'd actually picked up something from me about the fine art of negotiation.

Because she was winning. She'd gotten me to reconsider. I mean, concerts are so not my thing. The only ones I'd ever been to were these eardrum-splitting fiestas over-crowded with random rowdies. But maybe the Cranber-ries drew a different crowd. And maybe Tai was right; maybe a change of scenery couldn't hurt right now. Duh, picking up pukers for SafeRides every Saturday night hadn't exactly landed me in a toast-free zone. No matter how many times I'd gotten my Jeep detailed, it still reeked from the Paul Deveres of the world.

But what would I wear to a Cranberries concert?

I turned on my computer and clicked to Alt.Outfits. It wasn't a web site I docked at often. When the outfits came up on the screen, I was reminded of why. They included faded 501s—with suggestions of where the rips should be. As if! I kept clicking the mouse. No, no, reject, reject. Okay, here's one. A scoop-necked baby-doll dress with a tight, tiny T-shirt underneath. Thigh-highs and Joan & David ankle-high lace-ups. Doable.

When we got there, my cyber effort was not totally wasted on the arena rats. Okay, so I was prepared for the crowd: It was the generic Duh guys, sporting shredded Z. Cavariccis, never-been-washed flannels, and scruffy Docs to the max. And I was prepared for the Cranberries. I'd even snagged a CD from one of my SafeRides pickups. But, hello? Tai and Travis forgot to mention there was an opening act, Desperate Cry for Help. That's what they called themselves. Five randoms of indeterminate gender, all head-to-toe leather and chains, neon hair, with body parts pierced that I didn't even want to think about. They made Tai's New York posse look like the *Full House* kids.

Travis started to say something about how cool was it to have these third-row seats, but his voice was rudely obliterated because Desperate Cry for Help had begun. I was instantly reminded of why this is not my scene. It was all screechy metal, loud enough to melt the speakers along with any brain cells that may have inadvertently been left functioning. I had no idea what they were singing about, something like, "Face me! Erase me! Smash Me! Hate me!"

Worst of all? Tai and Travis were singing along! Fists punching the air, along with the rest of the brain-dead derelicts in the crowd, they were all, "Dirt! Slime! It's all sublime!" I knew I should probably have given it more of a chance, and I did try to stick it out. But my head was throbbing, and it wasn't in time with the beat. Okay, so I knew it would be rude to be totally Audi, but I had to do a lap. My survival was at stake. I leaned over to Tai and screamed at the top of my lungs, "I'm going to the ladies room!" She had no idea what I'd said but continued bopping, punching, stomping, and singing. Tai wouldn't even know I left.

"Excuse me, excuse me," I shouted as I started to fight my way out of the row. Everyone was all standing and shouting and totally oblivious to me, even as I stepped on my seventh pair of Docs and one metal-toed Sketchers boot. Finally, I got to the end of the row and breathed a sigh of relief. Whew! I'd made it in one piece.

Or had I? For just as I turned to head for the exit, this humongous herd of unruly generics came stampeding down the aisle straight at me, all screaming what sounded like "Mosh pit! Mosh pit!"

Quickly, I tried to dart back into my row, but it was too late. The mob was on top of me, pushing me forward—and then down. I was being trampled! I was screaming and sweating profusely. I couldn't breathe. I felt all these grubby hands all over me, and my life flashed before my eyes. Above the din of "Mosh pit! Mosh pit!" I heard the horrific sound of my dress starting to rip. Just before everything went black, I suddenly had this feeling of being lifted by one pair of strong, sure arms. I was rising, high up above the mob. A familiar voice seemed to be calling to me. I tried to answer, "I'm here! I'm here!" but nothing came out.

"Cher! Cher! Come on, baby, can you hear me?" I felt something cold and wet on my forehead, and something else, warm and tender, stroking my hair. My eyes fluttered open. Josh.

"What hap-hap-happened?" I managed weakly. "Where am I?"

Josh looked scared. Even in my state of semiconsciousness, I could also tell he looked really, really good. But his forehead was all crinkled and his face was clouded with concern. "You were in the wrong place at the wrong time. You got trampled in the mosh pit," he explained, gently brushing my hair out of my eyes. "We're in the first-aid station now." He was way soothing.

A paramedic stopped by and leaned over the stretcher I was apparently on. "She okay?" he asked Josh. "I think so," Josh said carefully.

"You rescued me?" I tried to sit up, but Josh gently pressed the ice pack back to my forehead and said, "Take it easy, don't try to get up yet. You've got a huge bump on your head." Truth is, the way he was holding and stroking me? I wasn't in any major hurry to change positions yet, anyway.

"What are you doing here, Cher? You were never into this scene. Have you really changed that much?" It occurred to me that Josh's questions were about more than just the concert.

And then I remembered why I *was* here—Travis and Tai were trying to occupy me and help me forget about him! I recovered enough to hoist myself up on my elbows. "It isn't me who's changed," I said with as much sarcasm in my voice as I could muster. Even though it did come out kind of pathetic-sounding. "And what are you doing here?" I challenged. "Even you wouldn't put up with Desperate Cry for Help."

"I was here for the Cranberries, and I was about to leave when I saw you being swallowed up by the mosh pit maniacs. I'm glad I was here. You could have gotten hurt badly, Cher."

"Why should my safety concern you?" I said, thinking, I already have been hurt badly—by you.

"I can't believe you would ask that," he said.

"Oh, yeah, well, I guess I am still Mel's daughter and all. That has to count for something with you." I tried to flip my hair, but my head hurt.

Josh was all quiet. Then he said, "You have always been much more than just Mel's daughter to me. You know that. And I don't know what happened while I was away, but I can take a hint—or a sledgehammer over the head, as you've preferred to handle it. It's obvious that you don't want to see me anymore. Maybe right now isn't the time, but I think I deserve an explanation."

"An explanation? You don't have to overtax your philoso-brain to figure it out, Josh. It's pretty obvious why I wouldn't want to see you anymore. Or do you think I'm really so clueless that I wouldn't find out?"

"Find out what, Cher? Listen, I don't know what to think. I go to Paris and first, you're writing me love letters and sending me cookies. And then without any warning or explanation, I stop hearing from you. And when I try to find out why, no one will give me a clue. You won't answer my calls or letters, De's suddenly taken a vow of silence, and Lucy's forgotten English." Josh was getting all indignant now—as if he were the injured party!

As breezily as possible—under the circumstances—I said, "I honestly don't know why this should be a problem for you, Josh. It isn't as if you spent your Parisian weekends all alone, is it?" At his puzzled expression, I added, "Does Out of sight, out of mind ring a bell, Josh? Or should I say Joshie?"

"I don't know what you're talking about Cher. You haven't been out of my mind for one second. All I do is think about you." Right, thinking of me and nuzzling her at the same time. Good trick.

"Well, maybe you should think a little harder, Josh. What possible reason could you have given me for breaking up with you?"

"None that I know of." And then he looked at me. The hurt in his eyes was palpable. Maybe he should switch his major to drama. He certainly had the aptitude for it. "You wouldn't believe some of the things I've been thinking. That you met some Armani'ed Romeo and he swept you off in his Rolls? Or that you were just too young for this kind of commitment? That you're just . . . fickle?"

Too young??!! Fickle??!! Not even!

"If anyone's fickle, it's you, not me," I shot back. "I know you found someone to replace me, so don't even try to lie about it. By the way, shouldn't you be getting back to her? I'm sure you didn't come to this concert alone."

"I didn't. I came with my fraternity brother Bob."

"Don't tell me. You left Ms. Nuzzle-Neck in Paris, and

now that you're in L.A. you want me back, is that it? Well, it doesn't work that way, Josh. I can't be just one of your girls."

He was getting totally flustered and all red in the face. Which I took to be a sign of guilt and embarrassment. But then he gently moved my legs out of the way a little, sat down on the stretcher, and took my hands in his hands. As calmly and seriously as I've ever heard him, Josh looked at me and said, "Cher, please tell me what's going on."

Okay, so I vowed that I wasn't going to give him the satisfaction of an explanation, but the way he looked at me? I couldn't help it. I pulled my hands away from his and lay back down on the stretcher. I looked away from him.

"I was there, Josh. I saw you and her." The memory of that awful day swooped down on me, and I could feel the tears welling up.

"Where were you, Cher?" Josh whispered, leaning in toward me and gently cupping my chin, forcing me to look at him.

"I came to Paris to surprise you," I said, sniffling. He looked way shocked. "I kept trying to find you, but you were always out—on some stupid field trip or at some dumb seminar. Dani and Pierre tried really hard to help me."

At the mention of Pierre, Josh's eyebrows shot up. "You met Pierre?"

I nodded and continued. "And he promised to get you to be around so I could surprise you. Except when I did see you, the joke was on me. I bought this whole new dress to surprise you in—and I was running to you, but suddenly you turned the other way, and she was all in your arms, and you were stroking her flannel shirt, and she was . . . nuzzling your neck. So I left before you could humiliate me any further. And then it rained. And to top it off, I was allergic to the dress and I got a rash!" I was full-on crying. Josh grabbed a gauze pad from the first-aid cart and started to dab at my face.

"Oh, Cher, Cher, is that what you've been thinking all this time?" He was all soft and gentle, as he closed his eyes and stroked my hair. "I can't believe you were there that day—talk about the worst timing, ever. If only you hadn't left. If only you'd come over to me. You would have found out right away that was just Jennifer Blakely."

And she would be . . . ? Josh bent down to kiss the top of my head, and explained, "She was one of the group that came over from UCLA with me. Do you remember I told you that in order to participate in this project, you had to keep your GPA above a 3.0? And if it dipped below, you'd have to leave the program and go back to L.A.?"

It sounded kind of familiar. I sniffled and nodded.

"Well, Jen had just gotten an express mail letter that she'd failed the econ midterm, and she was out. She had to go back to L.A. What made it really devastating was that she'd fallen in love while she was there with Sven, a Swedish student at the dorm next door. Jen was broken-hearted and came running out to me. I was comforting her, Cher, trying to calm her down. You would have done the same thing for a friend." Josh added, "She left for L.A. the next day."

I couldn't believe what I was hearing. All this time, I'd thought Josh had turned into some low-life two-timer, and all this time he didn't know what to think. "I can't believe you came all the way to Paris, Cher. If only I'd known you were there! We could have had such a romantic time and avoided all this heartache."

"So she really didn't mean anything to you?" I had to hear him say it one more time.

Josh looked at me and smiled. "As you would say, Cher, not even!"

And then Josh showed me what he meant, his way. He pulled me up into his arms, and gave me the longest, deepest, most passionate kiss in all of teendom. It made up for everything, and more.

In the background I could hear the Cranberries. They'd finally come on and they were playing that one song I knew, "Dreaming My Dreams."

Josh said, "You feel strong enough to dance, Cher?"

"Actually, I feel a little weak in the knees if you know what I mean, Josh. But yeah, as long as you hold me up if they start to buckle."

I put my head on his chest, and he held me and we danced. It was way better than actually being at the concert. Okay, so my makeup was all trashed, my dress was ripped, I had a bump on my head the size of Cleveland, but in every other way, it was just like that perfect dream I had. Except it was real.


The next day, when Josh rang the bell, I came flying down the stairs, ready to plant a big one on his lips. Lucy and Daddy were totally confused. Josh had come to bring me the present he'd gotten for me in Paris, a bottle of Trésor perfume. "I wanted to get you something authentically French," he said. He'd also brought trinkets for Daddy and Lucy.

Just then a FedEx truck drove up. "A delivery for Ms.

Cher Horowitz," the driver said, hauling a huge package out of the back. I snuck Josh a look—you got me something else? You sweetie! But he shook his head, No, it's not from me.

I examined the label. The return address said Paris, but I didn't immediately recognize the signature. "Open it, Cher," Daddy said. "Let's not keep us all in suspense. I've got work to get back to."

I ripped open the box and pulled away the bubble wrap. Inside was a framed portrait, almost the same size as the one of my mom hanging in the living room. Only this one was . . .

"Wow! That's beautiful, Cher, it looks just like you!" Josh was way impressed. "I guess I wasn't the only one who made a friend in Paris. Who's it from?"

I opened the card. It read, "To the best t.b. anyone could have, in the entire global village. All our love, Dani and Jean-Michel."

Daddy stared at the portait. I thought for a sec he was gonna say something way heavy, but instead he was all, "Well, I know where that's going. We'll move the portrait of your mother over and put yours right next to it. Then I'll be able to look at the two most important women in my life every day."

Impulsively, I ran over to Daddy and gave him a huge hug. And then I turned to Josh and fell into his arms. And then he kissed me. Maybe my first love *is* my truest love after all. At least that's how it feels right now.

# About the Author

Randi Reisfeld is the best-selling author of *The Kerrigan Courage: Nancy's Story* (Ballantine, 1994), as well as over a dozen books about young celebrities. Available from Archway Paperbacks is the exciting biography *Joey Lawrence*. She has also written *Meet the Stars of Melrose Place* and *So You Want to Be a Star!: A Teenager's Guide to Breaking into Showbiz*. Her *The Stars of Beverly Hills, 90210: Their Lives & Loves* has been translated into a dozen foreign languages, as has *The Official Baywatch Fact File*. Books for adults include *The Bar/Bat Mitzvah Survival Guide* and *When No Means No: A Guide to Sexual Harassment*, which she co-authored. Her most recent book is *This Is the Sound: Today's Top Alternative Bands* (Aladdin, 1996).

As Editorial Director of *16* magazine, Ms. Reisfeld has interviewed and written about the most popular stars of television, movies, and rock 'n' roll. Her articles have appeared in *The New York Times*, *Scholastic*, *First for Women*, and *Women's World Magazine*. Additionally, she writes a celebrity column for *Chatterbox*, a BBC publication in Great Britain.